Predisposed

A fictional novel

BY

Robert M. Tansley

The Key Publishing House Inc.

© Robert M. Tansley The Key Publishing House Inc.

All rights reserved. No part of this publication may be reproduced, stored in a retrieval system, or transmitted, in any form or by any means, without prior written permission. Any person who does any unauthorized act in relation to this publication may be liable to criminal prosecution and civil claims for damages.

First Edition 2010
The Key Publishing House Inc.
Toronto, Canada
Website: www.thekeypublish.com
E-mail: info@thekeypublish.com

ISBN 978-1926780-01-6

Copyediting & proof reading Jennifer South
Cover design & typesetting Velin Saramov

Library and Archives Canada Cataloguing in Publication is available

Printed and bound in Canada. This book is printed on paper suitable for recycling and made from fully sustained forest sources.

Published in association and a grant from The Key Research Center (www.thekeyresearch.org). The Key promotes freedom of thought and expression and peaceful coexistence among human societies.

The Key Publishing House Inc.
www.thekeypublish.com
www.thekeyresearch.org

Table of Contents

Chapter One - Memory 5

Chapter Two - Coffee 11

Chapter Three - Good Beginnings Lead to Good Endings. Bad Endings Lead to More Bad Ending. 17

Chapter Four - The Nut House 23

Chapter Five - Despair is a Colour not a Feeling 31

Chapter Six - Anger is a Feeling but Rage Takes Real Creativity .. 37

Chapter Seven - Not All Running is Exercise 47

Chapter Eight - Even the Hippies Became the Yuppies 52

Chapter Nine - Hope, Dope & How to Cope 58

Chapter Ten - Relief by Definition is Temporary 66

Chapter Eleven - Kaboom! 71

Chapter Twelve - The Horror of Life 76

Chapter Thirteen - The Cavalry 84

Chapter Fourteen - Grass in the Kitchen 88

Chapter Fifteen - Wanna Bet..93

Chapter Sixteen - Despair is the Absence of Hope......................100

Chapter Seventeen - Ink...103

Chapter Eighteen - Sparta.. 111

Chapter Nineteen - The Sperm Donor......................................122

Chapter Twenty - Surf and Turf...126

Chapter Twenty-one - Betrayal..133

Chapter Twenty-two - Searching..144

Chapter Twenty-three - Connect the Dots.................................150

Chapter Twenty-four - Revenge...157

Chapter Twenty-five - The Circle Closes 167

Chapter One

Memory

The past is never dead,
it is not even past.
– William Faulkner

"You are slumming today doctor. You are really on the wrong side of the tracks. Of course I have memories. I just doubt they are like your memories. We are galaxies apart you and I. I am not your typical patient, the anxious stay at home mother with some mild depression looking for Prozac to brighten up her day. You, you probably have wonderful memories with white sand beaches, smiles, sunshine, new bicycles and Frisbees. You probably have memories of birthday parties with balloons, streamers, piñatas, hugs, puppies and wrapping paper. There are clear lakes with docks, boats and laughter. When you think about those moments you feel good inside, warm, loved, attached, safe and secure. These are things that I have never had, never felt, never experienced. I wish I had your memories. I don't."

"My memories are like a completely shattered mirror with thousands of tiny shards of glass. Each little piece is a vague reflection, a memory, obscured, clouded, without focus and for good reason. They don't exist in any order or chronology. They sit in my head like an explosion with shrapnel and a debris field. The feelings attached to these memories are terror and pain, to be avoided if not totally suppressed. I have hidden these memories, buried them with self harm, substances, crisis, prescriptions and narcotics. I have hidden them from myself and from people like you. I have hidden them, run from them, avoided them, even denied them, for years."

"I suppose you want to hear one. No, I'm sorry, you need to hear one. You won't be happy until I tell you at least one, right? Isn't that how this works, free association, talk about whatever comes to my mind. I don't think you're ready. I think you're scared. I bet sitting in this lovely office you have listened to stories about infidelity, betrayal, maybe some blood has been spilled here in this perfect oak room with the frosted glass, plush carpet and the antiseptic smell of pine-sol. This office that is so safe, so high, away from the street with the security controlled elevator, security guard, soft music in the waiting room, the little fake waterfall and the nice magazines promoting better sex and larger penis size. And there is the rub. We both have to be here. If I am not here, I am on the street, out of the shelter, homeless. I am here against my will. They are forcing me to come here. It is in my contract for residency. Does that make you feel good, to know I don't want to be here, but I am here anyway? Do you enjoy that power?"

"OK dear Doctor, here you go, but I want to look at your face, while I tell this story. When your eyes recoil in disgust I will stop. I will see it, the subtle eyebrow drop. It's a test of sorts. I give you, maybe, twenty minutes before you are so sickened by my story that you vomit in your mind. It has to be on the inside because you are not real on the outside. You are a fake. You will glance over at your degree there on the pretty coffee coloured wall and you will think, 'holy fuck, this person needs help'. Then you will realize, 'oh, yeah, that's why she is here. That's what I am supposed to do', but all those nice polite university lectures didn't prepare you for the real world, for my world, the slum, the streets. The nice textbooks, the role playing, the well adorned classrooms, the rich bitch classmates, the rule filled campus, the well planned hazings gave you nothing. Your manicured hands, your expensive hair cut, the polished shoes and pleated pants are a dead giveaway. Did you take me on pro bono as a favour to the fuckers at the shelter? Or does your profession require you to take on a free hard case a month? Say something you fucking prick! Did you read my file? What does this one say, paranoid, borderline personality disorder, depression with anxiety features? I am tired. Can you prescribe meds? Can you write a 'script? I need some perc's. My back is killing me. It's an old injury, please."

"I know what you will write in my file; non-compliant, resistant; not amenable to treatment. And, bang, I am out on the street. I have met your kind before, self justifying, misguided, naive, distorted benevolence, blaming the patient when you fail. What happened to you? Couldn't live up to daddy's expectations? He wanted you to be an engineer?"

"Here is one of those mirror shards, a moment in my history. I remember the trailer, the trailer park, Boomtown. It is outside of Allentown in a little village called Ivan. I am maybe ten years old. The trailer is rank. It smells of urine, rotten food and human feces. There is a bed at one end where my grandfather sleeps. It's a sponge foam bed, stained, with an old tartan flannel sleeping bag on top. I sleep on the floor, on a blanket in what is the kitchen. I can touch the aluminum door that goes outside on one side and the cupboards that hold the sink where I sleep on the other. Anyone moving in the trailer steps over me. Someone coming in, steps over me. Someone going out, steps over me. Someone going to the bathroom, has to step over me. It's narrow. My feet are near the toilet. It's not really a room because there is no door. It doesn't qualify as a room if there isn't a door. In fact it's not really even a toilet because there is no running water attached to it. It is simply a hole out to another hole dug under the trailer. We have no running water. There are pails, with water. Beyond my feet is the television area with a bench where two people can sit and watch the television. When my mom is there, she curls up on that little bench to sleep. But, she is not there much. The trailer is filthy, dark. The little sliding windows are covered with sheets so no one can see in. And then there are the sounds."

"On this night there is a radio playing music. On this particular night I remember Johnny Cash. Can I sing for you?"

'I lie awake at night and wait 'til you come in.
You stay a little while and then you're gone again.
Every question that I ask, I get a lie, lie, lie.
For every lie you tell, you're gonna cry, cry, cry.
You're gonna cry, cry, cry and you'll cry alone,
When everyone's forgotten and you're left on your own.
You're gonna cry, cry, cry.'

"The TV is on, too, I can hear Gilligan's Island. The Professor is trying to teach Ginger something. It is theatre playing to no one. Laugh tracks and giggles to contrast this shit hole we live in. I can hear the traffic from the highway, the dull roar, the odd horn, a siren. And then there are the sounds I must listen to, pay attention to."

"I can hear the beer bottles hitting the table beside my grandfather's bed. There is no other sound like beer bottles bouncing off each other. The pitch tells me how full they are, how empty they become. They clank together. Some nights they fall to the floor. I pretend I am asleep as my grandfather steps over me. He is stumbling to the toilet. I hear him urinate. I hear his grunting and rasping, old man sounds. I am still, like death, barely breathing. I am trying to be invisible. It is so intense, terrifying that I feel myself crack, split. I detach myself from myself. I imagine I am somewhere else. I am someone else. It is no longer me on that cold floor. It is some other little girl."

"My matted blonde hair is greasy. I am allowed one cold shower a week. My face is not pretty. My crooked teeth have never seen a dentist. They are dirty, two are missing."

"It's random. It's not every night. Most nights he simply passes out, drunk. Then I sleep. I know the sound of that sleep, the snoring, the apnoea-filled gasps for air. But, this night, is not that kind of night. It's the mumbling, the almost incomprehensible, faltering speech. The content is bitter, angry, blaming and I am on the list. I can hear the intoxicated thinking spilling out of him. I am in the way, an inconvenience, a mistake, a burden, a waste of good sperm. Tonight, tonight I am past even that degrading description. Tonight I am 'that little cunt'. It's that kind of night we are having. I remain motionless hoping, praying to God, that he just steps over me and passes out. It would be a good outcome to the evening if I just had to listen to him masturbate. It's not that kind of night though."

"My grandfather is in his sixties. He is a miserable, horrible excuse for a man. His face is weather worn, wrinkled beyond his years. His brown eyes are sunken, drawn and bloodshot. The nose is pocked with alcoholic acne, sunken from years of glue and gas sniffing. His teeth are dark, nicotine stained. His breath smells like a sewer. He always has several days of beard growth, grey and black. There is almost no hair on his head. What he has is grey, uncut in a greasy comb-over. He is very overweight from a life time of bad eating, alcoholism and diabetes."

Pausing, I smile at the doctor and suggest, "You look nervous now Doc. Your Dr. Phil forehead is wrinkled in a perplexed kind of way. Your eyes are getting smaller. Your lips are squeezing in. I can see it in your face, your mind is filling in the blanks, anticipating what is next. You don't want to hear it but at the same time, you need to hear it. It's professional voyeurism. This is like sex to you, slowly opening me up to see what's in there. Don't look away. Look at me. Look at my face. Look at my eyes. Honour my story you freak. Don't look at your clock. You fuck! You are hoping our time is up. You are not ready to swallow my psyche, my being, my person. You want to spit me out. I will stop. You are not ready. Go back to school you incompetent fuck or is it Grand Rounds at the Hospital to keep your licence. I will go back to the shelter. I think you missed the lecture on the under belly of the world we live in. The world we all know exists but we don't want the messy details. I know your rationalizations, your bias. It's only in the big cities. It's a function of urban decay. You believe it's not in your neighbourhood, your schools, your town, your Allentown and you think I live in denial. In school I am sure that you had classes about poverty, hunger, oppression, lack of opportunity, democratically created alienation. It is all so polite and clean on PowerPoint."

"Goodbye Doctor. I will see you next week. I have to, to keep my spot at the shelter. You write your notes there. Make sure you say that I agreed to return. What do you think? I have an anxiety disorder with paranoid components to my personality? Should I be taking medication? Don't prescribe me too much, I am suicidal you know. You should know what I think. You deserve the truth. You are invisible to me. You are not really here. I have seen so many of you. Psychologists, psychiatrists, social workers, community workers, you all sound the same. A little tip for you, you don't really help anyone. You wasted seven years in medical school. Goodbye, Doctor."

As I leave I think I have been too harsh, but this goof is not the one. He is not the one to tell the truth to so I protect myself. I push him away, dismiss him with sarcasm, belligerence and hate. I put him in his place and I am in my place, alone, safe. Alone, I cannot be betrayed.

Chapter Two

Coffee

The most authentic thing about us is our capacity to create, to overcome, to endure, to transform, to love and to be greater than our suffering.
– Ben Okri

As I arrive back at the shelter the overweight day counsellor, Janice, greets me with, "How was your session with Dr. Colby, Margaret?" Janice is my primary worker—a designation that she holds that gives her power over me. She is my case manager because clearly I cannot manage my own life. It needs to be managed by someone, other than me. Janice weighs in at about two hundred and twenty pounds on her five foot five frame; she is big. She has eaten her hatred of men. She keeps herself safe with layers of fat. She has that, 'I never want to have sex with a man again' hair cut. The radical, short. gel-spiked hair and comfortable shoes tell me she is a lesbian. I don't even know her, but I hate her.

I lie to Janice, a lot, like this. "It was a good session. I think I made some progress today." This is what they want to hear. Later Janice will bully me into signing a release so they can speak directly with the therapist. It will be framed as good case management, so they can better plan my care at the shelter. For as much as they profess a flat hierarchy, a balance of power, respect, they will force me to do things I have no desire to do. They are hypocrites shining with good intentions about what is in my best interests. The problem is that they don't even know me. How could they possibly know what is in my best interests?

The shelter is a prison built with well-written Mission Statements and colourful Values, wrapped in strategic planning. There are no bars on the windows or locks on the doors to keep me in but it is a prison none the less. Their bars are built of no choices, guilt, shame, remorse, designed to keep me in. It is a sorority run by angry lesbians united in their hatred of men. To them, we are victims, forgiven our sins because we have been abused by men. As victims we are a commodity. They seek us out, recruit us. They patrol the soup kitchens, street corners and court rooms. It's legitimized stalking. They call it outreach. We are the pathway to more funding, higher salaries. I am a celebrity to them, because my file is over an inch thick, full of reports. It follows me like a ball and chain to these agencies. It is called electronic medical record keeping, designed to stop doctor shopping, cheating the system. The thicker your file, the more value you have to the shelter. The contents of my file are an open secret, this highly confidential information. We don't discuss it, the hospitalizations, the suicide attempts, the multiple diagnoses, the homelessness, the foster homes, the abuse. We all have the same information but we dare not discuss it, not in the shelter. I know they read the file like a novel, on the night shift when there is nothing to do, they read it, cover to cover. I can tell because the next morning I am treated like Michael Jackson, a super star, but at the same time, an absolute freak. I will become their star, for presentations at conferences, to get more money out of the United Way, the government, or a Rotary Club. My story plays the heart strings like a Philharmonic cello. I am a finely-tuned instrument for attracting money. I am female, homeless, orphaned, functionally illiterate, with a psychiatric history, a victim of both child abuse and spousal abuse; I cross at least three funding silos. I can get them one hundred thousand dollars in new annualized funding but I don't qualify for welfare. That's the system. They get rich off of me, bigger salaries, bigger benefits, bigger mortgages, bigger holiday packages and I eat out of garbage cans in alley ways.

Back in my room on my institutionally strong bed, bolted to the wall I can close the door and be alone. I will be given about twenty minutes before someone will check on me. It will be a polite knock and the door will open. The voice will say, "You OK Margaret?" It's a suicide watch. No one will admit that or discuss that with me but it is what it is. They need to keep their star resident alive. It's one of the ways that I know they read my file. I am a risk, a high risk. I fit the suicide profile, previous attempts, suicidal thinking, means and motivation. I see them counting the cutlery in the kitchen after every meal. There are no lamps in my room with cords, no sharp pens or pencils, no bed sheets. It's all so homey, just like in the brochure I picked up at the health clinic.

Dead, I am a huge liability. I am a public inquest waiting to happen, all that being said, I am taken care of very carefully. If I share one fake tear, I will be given the world. I can get a lawyer, a doctor, a dentist, a therapist, a social worker, a psychiatrist, medication on a moment's notice. I can jump the queue on any waiting list, straight to the front of the line. I have incredible, magical, powers for someone so powerless.

Here, at the shelter, I can clean up though, shower, eat, reflect, catch my breath, heal the wounds of the street. On the street life is not even day by day. It's meal to meal, fix to fix. It's like walking through a mine field, seeing death, dismemberment on every street corner. Awake all night, sleeping during the day. On the street we have nicknames, labels. It prevents us from getting attached to one another. I am Skully. I am forty-six years old but that has to be confirmed, even by me. To most, Skully is a reference to my hairless head. A combination of poor nutrition and anxiety has me wearing a wig, a ratty clump of fake hair. It serves other purposes too. I live in alley ways, behind dumpsters, in tent cities, under bridges, in door-ways, crack houses. I am the infamous NFA—no fixed address. I am that person you walk past as you stare and feel pity, a bag lady. At five feet two inches tall and ninety-two pounds I almost meet the criteria for anorexia. I am not on a hunger strike, with body image issues. My weight is a function of poverty, living on the street and substance abuse. I would rather get high than eat. My tattoos are badges of honour. I am inked from head to toe, sleeved. The sleeves hide my cutting, my suicide attempts, my tracks of substance abuse. I have a tattoo of a vine that starts at my right ear and wraps around my body seven times before it reaches my left ankle. I have a tribal tattoo on my left shoulder. Each tattoo has a story. They define moments in time in my life. It's like a permanent pictorial diary, like drawings you would find in a cave.

Today is team meeting day at the shelter. The staff will sit together at a board room table with donuts, coffee and talk about us behind our backs. It is the epitome of disrespectful. They will review my file. Every day my primary worker writes a report on my conduct in the shelter. I know what it says, "Margaret continues to be disengaged from the other residents. She remains withdrawn, distrustful. Suicide watch continues. Therapy is a condition of residency." After the meeting, Janice will ask to meet with me. She will discuss what they call my 'plan of care'. It is all pretty bizarre. I have been on the street for three years this time, eating garbage, in soup kitchens, sleeping in doorways and now I can't take a shit without a memo. If they only knew.

The shelter has eighteen beds. It is new. There must have been a building boom for shelters. It is in a lovely treed neighbourhood, hidden. It's location is a secret. There are no signs on the lawn or the door. They take women and children, no men. No men live there, work there or even visit there. They are so hateful of men, if they need a plumber, it has to be a woman. It's the No Men On Site Policy. The shelter is always full and beyond. I keep to myself. I have my own room, the VIP treatment. This is my second week at the shelter and I am getting annoyed. It is over-crowded and people are in my face too much. On the street I cope through mobility, moving, never feeling trapped. It's all too intrusive. Everyone is poking at me, asking questions. The staff, here at the shelter, compete over me. Each one thinks they will be the one to reach me, to connect with me, to organize my salvation. They all want to be the hero. I just want three hots and a cot. I want to be left alone. I can play the game for a while but it is grating on me. They have no idea who I am, really. I suffer from diagnostic confusion. I have been called paranoid, delusional, schizophrenic, depressed and anxious. You have to love professional name calling. My history includes three lengthy hospitalizations, psychiatric hospitalizations. One of my claims to fame is that I received ECT, Electroconvulsive Therapy during a hospital stay. I am a nut case. The odd thing is that I can really only see what is right in front of me, just beyond my nose. That is as far as I can cope. I don't look back. I don't look ahead. I barely function in the here and now. It is a dangerous place to be because I am unpredictable, unstable. My behaviour is not predictable. I don't have the filters other people do. The shelter has no idea how risky I am, living right under their noses. I don't even know, why I do what I do. I look like a little waif of a thing, skinny, tiny really, soft, placid, harmless. Today, I am going to snap and give them a glimpse of who I really am.

I have triggers, things that set me off. It's a function of post-traumatic stress disorder. I come by this honestly. Today my biggest trigger will be pulled and I will go off, violently.

The kitchen is a sort of gathering place. The coffee pot is there. Residents sit at the kitchen table and kibitz. The therapy session with Dr. Colby has scratched at an old wound of mine and I am on edge. Coffee is the last thing I need but there I am, shaking, coffee pot in one hand, cup in the other hand, in a protective zone, pouring away. Then the zone is shattered, my personal space invaded. All these ingredients represent a recipe for disaster.

My face is to the kitchen cupboards. They are lovely, with brass handles, in grain oak wood. So, then it happens, I am standing there with the coffee pot in one hand, my cup in the other hand. Suddenly, without warning, without permission, there is a hand on my shoulder. I don't even hear the words although I know something was said. It happened so fast no one could witness the true meaning of the event. No one was really watching. I turn and smash the coffee pot on the face of some bitch. She goes down hard, hot coffee on her breasts. Her scream is piercing, then there is silence. She is out, unconscious. I step over her and walk through the chaos. I shut out the bedlam and in a detached indifference go to my room and lay on my bed.

Someone will come. They always do. I will get a free pass on this one though. It's assault, maybe even assault with a weapon or assault causing bodily harm. The shelter only calls the police when an upset man shows up demanding to see his wife. They want him arrested, outside. The police do not respond well to issues inside the shelter. They believe with all their funding, all their staffing, the shelter should manage their own issues. Besides, the shelter cannot control whether it is a male or female police officer that attends.

Janice, my primary worker, comes to my room. She wants to know what happened. I can tell from her tone that she blames herself for my violent outburst. She believes that somewhere in that one inch thick file, there is the information that should have predicted and prevented this event. I don't even hear the story of the injuries, the facial lacerations, the burns to the skin, the concussion. The skank I smacked has gone to the hospital and will not return to the shelter. This is part of my power, my wizardry. I function with some odd immunity. I am somehow untouchable. I am rarely held accountable for my behaviour. In this place, in this environment, here, I am pure Teflon, nothing sticks to me. It makes one wonder. What has to be in place? What belief system must exist, such that I can smash a woman in the face with a hot coffee pot and nothing happens to me? It seems almost inconceivable but this is not the first time or the first place where I have gotten away with murder. Janice is going to ramble on about my contract with the shelter, my conditions of residency but in the end, nothing will happen to me. I have been chewed out before. This only makes me stronger. It gives me more power, more options.

Chapter Three

Good Beginnings Lead to Good Endings

Bad Endings Lead to More Bad Ending

Life's challenges are not supposed to paralyze you, they're supposed to help you discover who you are.
– Bernice Johnson Reagan

Back in the therapist's office I know the coffee pot incident report has been faxed to the doctor. He won't be passive today. He won't be allowing me to free associate, to ramble on. Now, he will have an agenda.

"Margaret," and so he begins, "I enjoyed meeting you last week and since our first meeting I have had a chance to read your file. You have really been through the system, foster homes, group homes, hospitals, detoxification centres, addiction treatment centres, a little jail time I see and shelters. You have quite the history. Your mother was murdered and your father too. You were raised by your grandfather, but he also died, when you were quite young. You have suffered a great many losses. Are you on any medications right now?"

I look the doctor up and down while I assess my options to determine a course of action. He is in his fifties, distinguished looking. He's no rookie, no resident in training. He's solid, for real. Sitting in his comfortable black leather chair holding his note pad he looks like a more hip Sigmund Freud. It must be a requirement, part of the criteria to get into psychiatry school, to look like a Freud knock off, with the little goatee, the bulging suspenders.

"No, no medications," I respond politely.

"When is the last time you were on a medication?" he asks.

I see where this is going. He has read the coffee pot report and thinks I need to be medicated to keep the people at the shelter safe. He is working for the shelter. They are paying his session fees. I love this. He wants to medicate me into a zombie-like state. Now it's play time for me. Once the therapist has an agenda, it's time for a little fun. He is not that good. A good therapist knows how to posture, how to position themselves relative to me and my position. Therapy is like judo, you need some momentum from the patient to develop an agenda. I have him right where I want him.

"I can't remember the last time I took a prescription medication. That doesn't mean I haven't been taking my medicine, if you know what I mean?" I offer up the bait. Psychiatrists are driven by the medical model, assess, diagnose and treat. He needs more information to make a diagnosis. It's pigeon holing driven by the bible of psychiatry, the DSM-IV-R. DSM stands for Diagnostic and Statistical Manual. I may be illiterate, but I am not stupid. When you spend time in institutions you pick some things up. The DSM contains all available diagnoses and the symptoms that make up those conditions. Psychiatrists do this thing called a Mental Health Status Exam. To justify a diagnosis they must prove specific criteria are met. They gather information related to your symptoms to complete the exam. The fun part is that you are the principle source of information. The fastest way to confuse a psychiatrist is to mix addictions and mental health together. It's a cocktail that disables, disorients a psychiatrist. This guy, Dr. Colby, is easy to play with. I am bobbing and weaving, avoiding, dodging, like Muhammad Ali in the ring with Joe Frazier, 'down goes Frazier'.

"Your chart indicates you have had quite a variety of medications, depression medications, medication for anxiety, even an antipsychotic drug," Dr. Colby searches.

"I also had different sleep medications. I have trouble sleeping. On the street, I usually drink myself to sleep. And pain medications, I have had a lot of pain medications." I am pleased with myself.

Dr. Colby flips through his notes. I can tell he is lost and then he surprises me. He says,

"Last week you were in the middle of a story and you stopped. I must say, that may have been my fault. I am sorry. I may have shut you down in some way. I would like to hear the rest of that story. It seemed quite compelling. We didn't get off to a good start. You were sleeping on the floor of your trailer. Your grandfather was there. It seemed he was drunk. Can you carry on with that story, please?" Now we have a chess match.

Now I am confused as to my next move. That was a nice recovery. He is off the medication train and the agenda to control my behaviour. Is he genuinely interested in me, my story? This is my vulnerability. I fall into this trap every time like a mouse staring at the cheese. I can't not respond to this level of curiosity, if it is sincere. At some level, I want someone to hear and believe my story. So I will throw him a bone with more of the story. I will drill this down and see how he responds. I am not sure what this is but it is at least a dilemma. There are things that have happened in my life that sit inside me like a time bomb. I need to let these things out but at the same time I am afraid that if I start I will not stop and melt into the floor.

I begin by saying, "I have been told my whole life that I am a mistake. I am in the way, that I should have been an abortion. I am no one, a nothing. And so there I am, ten years old, on the floor of the trailer, in my grandfather's care. My mom is off with her latest man and she doesn't want that ruined, by me. I see her maybe once a month. I go to school maybe half the time. The rest of the time I am in the trailer and trailer park."

The doctor interrupts, "I get all of that Margaret, but what happened that night, when you were on the floor, in the trailer? There were a lot of things you could have said in our first session, but you chose that particular event to discuss. What happened that night?"

I respond, "Well," with a long pause, as I stare intently at Dr. Colby, "I just wanted to, to tell you, it was rough."

Dr. Colby is not impressed and responds, "Margaret, I know you don't yet trust me. It's hard to just meet someone and spill your guts. You're checking me out. I get that, but let's not waste each other's time. Are you here to do work or jerk me around?"

I am thinking now! I have never heard that out of a psychiatrist before. This isn't the usual, 'tell me more about that' therapy. Still, I am not ready to open up Pandora's Box.

I deflect again by changing the subject. "Did they tell you about the coffee pot?"

The doctor responds. "Yes, I read the incident report. They faxed it to me. Would it be easier to discuss that?"

He has me on the run. He knows I am deflecting and he is challenging me. This guy is good, by saying, 'easier', he is appealing to my ego, suggesting I am taking the easy way out.

The doctor continues, "Listen Margaret, I am interested in helping you. I have read your file. You have been through hell. I can't even pretend to think I know what you must feel. I don't. But this I do know. We can visit weekly while you are in the shelter and shoot the shit or we can do some real work. This is either an opportunity or a joke and it's up to you to decide. I get paid the same either way. You signed a release so I can talk to the shelter, but my guess is that they forced you to sign it. I will rip it up if you wish. Here it is. What shall it be? You don't have to decide today and it is

your choice. Honestly, I don't care. You decide. I will see you next week. We can talk about the weather or we can resolve some issues."
    I leave this appointment pretty confused. I have not seen this type of behaviour from any of the helping professions. A psychiatrist, prepared to rip up a signed release of information is a rare animal. My reflections are all over the map. I am getting older. This is changing my view of the world. I am tired, troubled, even tormented by things I have seen, done. A force is growing in me to purge myself of certain memories, certain feelings. This compulsion makes me feel vulnerable, exposed. I could be building my own gallows.
    Back at the shelter, I am in my room considering my options. I find this quite stressful. It creates racing thoughts in my head, a state of confusion, distress that makes me crazy. Memories are flashing in my head, darting across my mind. It impacts every inch of my body. My hands shake, my legs twitch, my stomach twists into knots. I feel like throwing up. The images in my mind are horrific and fleeting. I see the charred body of my grandfather, my mother's lifeless eyes, blood. My breath is now short, rapid, I am in a full blown panic attack. I feel trapped, my chest compressed and at the wrong place, the wrong time Janice, my primary worker walks in the room. I am on my bed shaking, twitching like I am having a seizure. My heart is pounding trying to escape my chest. My eyes are rolling back in my head. I feel that I may pass out. I can hear Janice screaming, "Call 911, call 911!" This draws a crowd, escalating my symptoms. I begin to convulse, my muscles cramp and I am stiff like a board. More screaming begins, "Do something, help her, do something, help her!" I pass out, covered in sweat. I have lost control and peed my pants.
    I wake up in the hospital. That environment is completely recognizable, immediately. I look around the room. I am on an intravenous drip. I try to focus on the bag to see what medication they have forced into my body. I realize that I am in restraints. My wrists are wrapped with a leather strap fastened to the hospital bed. My ankles too are fixed. As I look around the room, I see I am not alone. The ward room offers me two room-mates. They are asleep. The window tells me that it is day time, what day remains a mystery. The hospital room adornment tells me that I am in the regular medical ward, not a mental health room. As I get my bearings I have this odd sensation that I am floating, euphoric, a dead

giveaway that I am on some form of opiate medication. I settle in for the ride. This is addict heaven, legal mind-altering substances, safely, medically prescribed and administered. It's magic. There is no point in fighting this high. I slip into a deep sleep. I am physically and chemically restrained.

Chapter Four

The Nut House

What do you think you are, for Chrissake, crazy or somethin'? Well you're not! You're not! You're no crazier than the average asshole out walkin' around on the streets and that's it.
— McMurphy,
"One Flew Over the Cuckoo's Nest"

I wake up to the friendly face of Doctor Colby. I smile and offer, "What are you doing here?"

He responds, "Checking on you."

"How am I doing?" I ask.

"Well, I removed the restraints. That did not seem necessary but you got the celebrity treatment," the doctor replies.

"Figures," I observe.

"How are you feeling?" he asks.

"I had a panic attack didn't I?" I ask.

"Seems so. Did our session upset you?" the doctor offers with worry.

"Yes," I agree.

"Are you ready to do some work? Your response is actually pretty healthy and tells me that there are issues that need attention. The panic attack is your mind's way of telling you to heal. Do you want to talk now?" the doctor asks.

"Not here," I nervously suggest.

"No, of course not, we can go to a private interview room if you want," the doctor suggests.

"Does my hospital gown have a back or is my ass hanging out?" I wonder.

"Definitely, ass hanging out, I will get you a robe," the doctor confirms.

In the interview room I am feeling impressed with Dr. Colby. He has come to see me in the hospital. I need to get my bearings, "What day is it and what hospital am I in?"

"It's Wednesday. You had your panic attack on Monday, so you lost a day. You are in Allentown General Hospital. They are holding your bed at the shelter," the doctor updates me.

I respond, shocked, "Holding my bed? That is unheard of. They are over capacity, all the time. After the coffee pot scene I thought they would be glad to be rid of me."

Dr. Colby replies, "They don't want you on the street. They don't want you homeless. They know the hospital will triage you and discharge you as quickly as possible. So, you don't have to worry about where you live. I don't want you going into survival mode. I know once you flip to day to day living, you won't have the strength, the emotional strength to focus on the issues that exist inside your therapy. Therapy requires a foundation because things get worse before they get better when you are uncovering emotional wounds that are not healed."

That is a really nice speech. However, the good doctor has no idea what he is dealing with. If nothing else he is persistent. He has no idea who I am. He has no idea what I have been through, what I have done, the life I have led. I am struggling. This is the scariest place on the planet for me. Every ounce of my being says run and I could. I have no fear of the street. I am comfortable there, safe. The doctor has it all backwards. I am not safe in the shelter or the hospital. I am safe on the street. On the street we have a code. We respect one another's privacy. No one is scratching away at your past, your history, your mistakes. Knives, guns, needles are nothing in comparison to someone digging away at you emotionally. At the same time, at some level, I know the doctor is right. I am not a kid any more. I feel this pressure to come to terms with my past, my mistakes. The doctor wants to hear the rest of the story about the trailer, my grandfather. He has no idea how deep that rabbit hole goes. It ends badly, very badly.

The doctor interrupts my reflecting, "Are you OK? The choice is yours."

I am moving this forward, "OK, OK, where was I?"

The doctor reminds me, "You were on the floor of the trailer pretending you were asleep."

And I am off, "Right. I am on the floor, terrified, being still, distracting myself, coping by fantasizing that I am not really there. I have split myself in half, emotionally. In my mind, I am sitting near a pond, with soft grass, willow trees and rabbits. The sun is shining. I can hear birds singing. It is a picture that I have drawn many, many times, literally. It is one of my coping mechanisms, drawing, sketching, art. I am detaching myself from the here and now. This is a skill I have developed over several of my young years. I will save that for later. At that moment I am on the floor, terrified, trying to cope. My drunk, miserable grandfather is urinating, grumbling. It's winter, the floor is cold. The trailer is heated by an electric heater at one end and a kerosene heater at the other."

"My grandfather, my grandfather, done urinating, steps over me as he leaves the bathroom and pauses. He has one foot on each side of me and he stops. I remain still. It seems like forever that he stands over me. Suddenly he bends down and rips my blanket off of me. My eyes jump open."

The doctor interjects, "Margaret, look at me. Margaret, look at me. You are shaking Margaret. Take a breath. Let's slow this down. That is really powerful. Margaret I don't want you to disappear into that story so I am going to ask you to do something. I want to keep you grounded while you tell your story. I want you to take the belt from your robe and hold it in your hands, squeeze it as you talk."

I become more aware. Aware enough to respond, "They won't give me a belt. I could hang myself with it."

"Good point, OK, use mine," the doctor offers.

Before he can move I shout, "NO! Don't take off your belt!"

The doctor is clearly unsettled and distressed, "What is it Margaret? Why are you upset?"

"The belt, leave it on. I can't. I can't." I am shaking again, staring at the doctor's belt.

The doctor tries to recover, "Oh my god. I am so insensitive. You have been sexually abused haven't you? The belt, the removal of the belt, it's a trigger, of course. I am so sorry Margaret. I must be brain dead. You must think that I am a rookie. It's a rookie mistake. I am sorry. That was a very bad idea."

I agree, "Yes it was, but I would like to continue. We have gone this far. I will hold this pillow if it helps. This is so hard." I pause for what feels like an eternity. I take a throw cushion from the couch, clutching it I continue. "I am on the floor of the trailer, that cold hard floor. I have been shocked out of my day dream. My grandfather is standing over me. I feel his feet squeeze my body. He has me pinned. I look up and I can see his testicles, penis, his large stomach hanging over me. I wiggle to try and escape. He grunts and tightens his grip with his feet. His heels are dug into my ribs on each side of my body. He is speaking but I can't understand the words." Again, I look briefly at the doctor. I have to stop talking. I am rocking back and forth rhythmically. "I look up again and he is squatting his butt closer to my face. I am trembling with fear. I close my eyes and I am working to turn myself off, to separate myself from what is happening. I am looking for my pond, my sunshine. This is hard. This is so hard. I can't say it."

The doctor helps, "It's OK Margaret, finish the story. You are safe."

I continue. "OK, OK, my grandfather, my grandfather, he, he, he defecates on my face."

There it is. It's out there now. Looking at Dr. Colby, I am crying, sobbing, wrenching with tears. There is silence, no response from the doctor. Fear grips me. I am terrified that I will flip this sadness to anger, rage. I can feel it boiling deep inside me. My eyes are darting around the room. I am looking for a weapon, something I can smash. I want to rip the room apart. I want to choke Dr. Colby out. I am in a homicidal rage, desperate to explode.

The doctor interrupts my developing fantasy, "Margaret. I am so sorry you had to experience that. That is the most horrific story I have ever heard. Your grandfather was a monster. There isn't anything more degrading, damaging psychologically than that event. It explains a great deal about you. How you have carried that memory around for all these years and still moved forward, I don't know. You have such courage, Margaret."

I don't respond. I am not expected to respond. My head is in my hands, slouched in the chair, a pillow on my lap, I am in a sick state of mind. Working to control my rage I am motionless like that little girl on the floor of that trailer. The doctor thinks he has me figured out. He sees me as a victim of child abuse. At ten years of age, he thinks such an event would ruin my psychological development forever. He has no idea what came before that event or what followed that event. That event is only one moment in time. It is one of those shards of broken mirror reflecting back to me, who I am. The doctor believes that this has defined me and it explains the self harm, the cutting, the hospitalizations, the medications, the diagnoses. He knows nothing. He has panicked. He is afraid to hear the rest of the story. I am going to force him to hear it, to swallow it, to own it.

"Doctor, what do you think happens next? There I am, on the floor, a little ten-year-old girl, pinned by her three hundred pound sweaty disgusting grandfather and I have shit, shit on my face. Where does that go? I will tell you where it goes. He laughs. He laughs. He steps back over me to wipe his filthy hairy ass off over the toilet, laughing. I am silently crying, frozen in terror. I don't know if this is over, or just the beginning. We are in that area that few people understand. They don't understand because they live inside a moral code, a naïve world. They imagine that even when something bad happens the person acting inappropriately catches themselves and withdraws. They know there may be a slap and then a recoil, regret, then apologies. They don't want to believe that for some people, that is just the beginning of the fun. I take my blanket and wipe the feces off my face. My grandfather steps over me again and crawls into his bed. I get up to wash my face. I am looking at myself in the mirror and wish I were dead. I roll up the sheet with the feces and throw it outside the trailer. I wash my face and I wash my face and I wash my face. I think I washed my face a hundred times as my grandfather slept. I know now, that it was at that moment that Skully was born. I am washing my face and pulling out my own hair. Skully did not have a name at that point but she had a personality, an emotional position in the world. I don't think I slept. It was a school night and I am going to go to school to get out of the trailer. Can you imagine being ten years old, walking to school, with that having been your night at home with your grandfather?"

"You arrive at school. Your friends see you and rush over to greet you and they ask, what did you do last night? I go to school." I go to school with these thoughts racing through my head. I am ruminating, stuck in a never ending feedback loop, transfixed by the abuse I have experienced as I contrast it with how my classmates may have spent their evening home with their families.

That is my story for the doctor but it is incomplete. The doctor will not ask for more because he has heard enough. He doesn't have enough courage or experience to ask if there is more, to drill this down further. It's not the whole story but I have to hold back. As I am washing my face, in the trailer, pulling out my hair I am obsessing, raging, fixated on the hate I have for my grandfather. In the morning, ready for school, I am staring at my grandfather. He is more unconscious than asleep, his hairy ass hanging out of the sleeping bag that only half covers him. I am ready for school, standing in the trailer. I am there for maybe ten minutes, staring, raging. I turn to leave for school and I see the kerosene heater. I pause. It is on the floor, near the television, the soft heat radiating from the unit. Staring at it my thoughts are confused, erratic. I am not sure how much intent was involved in this. I wasn't sure what would happen, what would be the ultimate outcome, but I kicked it over. It was a quick, deliberate kick. My tiny foot, in my tiny winter boot reached out and kicked the kerosene heater over. It was like I might kick an empty pop can in a parking lot as I walk to school. I didn't really feel anything. There was no rage, anger, in that moment. It was a disconnection from my rage, a moment of silent clarity. The heater fell over, I turned and I stepped out of the trailer with the sound of the aluminum door closing, ringing in my head. I didn't look back until I was about a block away. I turned around and looked at the trailer. It looked the same. It was not engulfed in flames or even on fire as far as I could tell. I thought, at that moment, it was completely possible, that nothing happened. Perhaps, I thought, the heater had a safety device in the event it was knocked over.

So, there I am at school, looking at all the other children in my class, wondering how their evening at home had been. Maybe they played Monopoly with their mom or went to figure skating lessons. I am pretty sure, confident in fact, that no one else was held down and shit on by their grandfather. The uniqueness of the story compelled me to keep it a secret. I am sitting in class with a familiar feeling, I don't fit in here. I don't belong here. No one wants me here. I am different from everyone else, here. We are that family, the poor family, the broken home.

I don't have a lunch. Back in class, after the lunch break, we are working on the times tables. It's about two o'clock and I see the principal at our classroom door. He walks in and whispers something to my teacher. My teacher glances at me with a worried look. Then the principal calls my name and motions for me to follow him. I have this odd feeling that this is the last time I will leave this classroom. We go to his office. There is a woman there, whose name I now cannot remember. She is a social worker from the Children's Aid Society.

We are sitting in the principal's office. They tell me that there has been an accident and that my grandfather is dead. They explain that there was a heater that caught fire and burned the trailer, my grandfather and all of our possessions. The social worker further explains that they cannot find my mother so I am going to a foster home. I am speechless; my first murder. I have taken my grandfather's life.

In the hospital, in our interview room, clutching a pillow, I don't tell the doctor any of this. He is feeling pity for me. Pity is power. I don't want to muddy the waters, by disclosing my murderous intent, actions. I can carry on the story and leave out the killing my grandfather part. No one blames me, accuses me, no one even suspects me. I can pick up the story being in foster care. After the story in the trailer, people expect you to end up in foster care. And there I am, in foster care.

I say to the doctor, "After that I am placed in a foster home."

He replies, "I should hope so Margaret. Can we pick this up next week in my office? I am going to get you discharged from the hospital so you can get back to the shelter. Is that a reasonable plan?"

I agree. "Yes Doctor. Thank-you."

Chapter Five

Despair is a Colour not a Feeling

Life is divided into the horrible and the miserable.
– Woody Allen

"Greg and Andrea Switzer, Greg and Andrea Switzer, let me tell you about Greg and Andrea Switzer. Greg and Andrea Switzer lived in a large five bedroom home on the outskirts of the City of Ivan, Ontario, the same Ivan where I lived with my grandfather in the trailer park. Ivan is truly a pimple on the ass of Ontario. It was the most beautiful home I had ever seen. The front door opened to a glistening ceramic tile floor that flowed to a sunken living room with the softest, most plush carpet my feet had ever felt. It was certainly the opposite side of the tracks to the trailer park where I lived with my grandfather. It was several miles outside of town on a number of treed acres of beautiful land."

"The Switzers were in their late fifties. They had three children of their own. Two of the children were in their twenties and lived on their own in the City of Allentown, thirty miles from Ivan. The remaining child was Lucas. He was eighteen and living at home with his parents, still in high school."

I am in my third session with Dr. Colby. I have shared one of my most horrific memories but left out one important detail. I kicked over the kerosene lamp catching the trailer on fire killing my grandfather.

I continue to tell my story to Dr. Colby. "This is my second time in a foster home. I was in care for three months when I was five years old. My mother was badly beaten by her boyfriend. She was put in hospital and I was put in a foster home. When my mom was released from the hospital she went back to her boyfriend. The Children's Aid Society would not let me go home. My mom chose her boyfriend over me. Soon after that Bobby, the boyfriend, was arrested and put in jail. When it was clear that Bobby would not be coming back for a while I went back to my mother's. She missed Bobby. She didn't miss me."

"It is a gross understatement to say that it was awkward getting dropped off at a foster home by a social worker. The car ride to the home was quiet. I am looking out the window, softly crying, counting the hydro poles, to distract my mind from the reality that I am ten years old, and no one wants me. The world looks very blurry through the tears of abandonment. Your mind races, thoughts, fantasies, that there is a rich uncle, a baron with a pony coming to save you. I comfort myself by counting hydro poles compulsively. I remember what was playing on the car radio. It was the Rolling Stones, "Sympathy for the Devil",

'Please allow me to introduce myself
I'm a man of wealth and taste
I've been around for long, long years
Stole many man's soul and faith

And I was 'round when Jesus Christ
Had his moment of doubt and pain
Made damn sure that Pilate
Washed his hands and sealed his fate

Pleased to meet you
Hope you guess my name
But what's puzzling you
Is the nature of my game'"

"Even the social worker seems to know this is an unnatural act. A brief stop at McDonald's Restaurant was designed to build my relationship with the social worker whose name I can't even remember. There is just no kind way to place a child with complete strangers, to live, because you are acknowledging that there is nowhere else for the child to go. For all the talk of family, family first, the system is slow, unresponsive. So, there I was in the Switzers elegant living room, eating a cookie, drinking a glass of milk with my whole life upside down. I had no one. There was no aunt or uncle or baron with a pony, on their way from a far away city to claim me, rescue me. That was the elephant in the room comforted with chocolate chip cookies, pleasant introductions and 2 percent milk. I have lost my grandfather, my school, my home, my mother. The Switzers were educated as to who I am. The Children's Aid Society has a file on me. I don't get a file on the Switzers. The Switzers could turn me down. I have no choice. I can't turn them down. It all takes about thirty minutes and the social worker leaves."

"Mrs. Switzer takes me to my room on the lower level of the

home. It is nice enough with a bed, dresser, desk, chair, with blue dimpled carpet and soft cream-coloured walls. There is a large window that does not open in any way, a clock and a large picture of a giraffe. It has been a long day. It started with heading off to school and learning my grandfather was dead. Now I am in a strange home, in a strange room with no idea what may be next."

"Mrs. Switzer takes me to a bathroom on the lower level where I shower, wash my hair and brush my teeth. They have new flannel pyjamas for me covered in little white bunnies. I crawl into the soft, warm bed and I fall into a fitful sleep of nightmares, terrors and disorientation. I awake in the middle of the night, having no idea where I am. I arrived literally only with the clothes on my back. I am ten years old and there is no sense of safety, security, attachment in my life. I feel unwanted, unloved, useless, pretty much how my grandfather described me. I was awake for a couple of hours but did fall back asleep."

"The next morning Mrs. Switzer wakes me up. She says there will be no school today so we can shop for new clothes. We have pancakes, orange juice, bacon and watermelon. I can't even remember the last time I had breakfast. I don't remember saying a word. I am eating like I haven't eaten in a month, wolfing down food, guzzling juice while the news plays on the local radio station. There is a story about a fire, a trailer and the death of an old man. At the kitchen table my eyes are darting around the room. This is a home, with fridge magnets, picture frames, knick knacks and a spice rack. The clean linoleum floor, the shiny sink fixtures and the bright white appliances reflect a care, an affection I have not seen before. Clearly someone loves this house, this home and the people that live in it. I am wondering what I am doing there. I am thinking that I don't fit in there. I am questioning why a family like this would want to take in someone like me. This is clearly not about money. The Switzers don't need the thirty dollars a day they will receive for caring for me. I know today that this is about avoiding attachment. I know this won't last and I can't settle in. I certainly can't develop any feelings for this family because history tells me this will all end so very badly. At ten years old, I already have a very negative world view. I have no thoughts or feelings of hope or optimism."

The doctor interrupts my story. "What makes you think you don't deserve to be in the Switzer's home?"

I respond, "Doctor, I am ten years old at that point. I have been raised in poverty, abuse, filth, degradation. I have been neglected, malnourished, beaten, violated. I am skinny, dirty, ugly, an urchin. I have already been in foster care once. I have attended five different schools. I have moved so many times I have lost count, maybe ten. My mother chose her boyfriend over me. I am not sure I deserve to be alive. One time my mother got pissed with me and tossed me, breaking my collar bone. She took me to the hospital and used the opportunity to go to Florida. She checked me in, left and took a plane to Florida. I spent a week in hospital when I should have been in and out after a few hours. I am seriously screwed up. To cope, to distract myself, I am developing ticks, obsessive thoughts and compulsive behaviours. I am drawing, faces mostly, faces with feelings. I am pulling out my own hair. I am counting, hydro poles, drips in the sink, holes in the ceiling tiles, squares on the linoleum floor. I am ten years old and I am seriously fucked up."

"The day with Mrs. Switzer was amazing. In town, we shopped and she knew everyone. She stopped in every store, shop, beauty salon and introduced me to everyone. She did it with such pride, genuine glee. I have a lot of one word answers but Mrs. Switzer is in some bizarre place treating me like pure gold. I am really confused. Where does such a person come from? She is so full of energy, positive emotion and outlook. There is no hesitation in this person, no caution, no worries. She is confident, proud and treating me like I am a princess. She bought me more clothes in a day than I had seen my whole life. Everything I liked, she bought. This was way past what Children's Aid Society would pay for. This was out of her pocket and she was pleased to be doing it."

"I will make a long story short here Doctor. Mrs. Switzer was a mother. She was like a professional mother, someone who was meant to be a mother, loving, kind, attentive but her role was coming to an end. I was a sort of snooze button to the empty nest. She had raised three children and she could see her days as a mother coming to an end. She couldn't accept that, couldn't have any more children of her own, so voila, I am the solution. Mrs. Switzer's youngest child, Lucas was eighteen. He didn't need nor want much mothering any more. Mr. Switzer was this hard working guy who accidentally became rich. He was in the right place at the right time and his little plumbing business exploded into a major corporation with forty trucks, a hundred employees and more money than they could spend in three lifetimes. It was a perfect fit, a match made in heaven. So, you have to wonder, how are the wheels going to come off here? It sounds perfect. I couldn't be in a better place, lots of love, lots of money, plenty of attention. You will have to wait until next week to hear the next chapter though, Doctor, our time is up."

The doctor replies, "You're right Margaret, our time is up. You are doing really well here. I am pleased that you have chosen to open up and tell your story. This is a great opportunity for you. The shelter is committed to you so you are safe, with housing, food and you can come here."

I exit with, "Thank-you Doctor." Dr. Colby is all right in my book but I can't tell him the whole truth. He thinks he has the whole story. He is a fool.

Chapter Six

Anger is a Feeling but Rage Takes Real Creativity

Endure the present and watch for better things.
– Virgil

Back at the shelter my three hundred pound lesbian case manager has that look in her eye like they have been talking about me behind my back again. It enrages me. They must have some brilliant ideas for what is in my best interests. Ideas generated without me present. This is going to be painful, for her. The weekly team meeting with doughnuts and coffee has sickened me again, on schedule. It would appear that my case has once again dominated the conversation I am sure. Case managers like to make referrals to other services. This way you are passed around like a hot potato in a matrix of agencies where ultimately no one is responsible for your treatment. It's perfect for when the wheels come off they can all blame one another. I have seen it all, group therapy, individual therapy, cognitive behavioural therapy, dialectic behavioural therapy, sexual assault centres, domestic violence shelters, A.I.D.S. outreach, family service agencies, community health centres, adult mental health centres. It's clear what is coming, an offer that I can't refuse, they think. That awkward little dance where they want me to agree but when I hesitate, they force me with their dark authority, the authority that is inside their flat hierarchy and deep respect for self determination.

Janice, in all her immenseness has me seated in a small meeting room, my back to the wall facing the only heavy door with a small crack of an unbreakable window. She takes the office chair with no arms so she doesn't get her fat ass stuck while she is seated. Janice is between me and the only door. I can tell by her micro reflexes that she is a smoker, big time. The lip twitching is a dead give away. She is in the middle of a huge nicotine craving driven by her anxiety. All this tells me that she is the bearer of bad news. The gel in her hair shines in concert with her round face. Her flowered dress is huge but still wraps tight around her hips and behind. She wears one of those industrial strength bras and her breasts still sag to her belly button. The tiny feet are covered with a ballet slipper making sure her rose ankle tattoo is visible. I imagine that she also has a tramp stamp on her lower back, probably a butterfly symbolizing her rebirth when she came out of the closet and embraced her sexual orientation. I know my tattoos. She looks really uneasy so I am confirming that I won't like what she has to say. A bead of sweat is running down her face near her ear. The walk down the stairs to the office has challenged her fitness level and she is perspiring. This can't be coming from Dr. Colby. He would discuss any recommendations with me first. I know him at least that well. He would not deliver bad news through the shelter staff. Janice fretfully begins, her voice cracking as she speaks, "We have a suggestion. You know we hold weekly team meetings to review cases. We think you should be in an anger management program. The coffee pot incident has generated some worry."

And there it is, the bad news, the bottom line. The worry Janice mentions are the staff. The staff are the royal we. The staff, the faceless, nameless, gutless staff is worried about their safety. I love it. Janice has been given marching orders by her colleagues to get me into anger management. My reaction is not good. I am conflict avoidant. I cope by moving away, running, that flight response. Here I feel trapped. Between me and the door are a table and that enormous bitch of a woman. The room is too small, like the trailer was too small. I can feel myself heating up, my muscles tightening up. My eyes are darting around the room and I go off. I quickly stand up pushing over my chair with a crash. In front of me is a figurine, a circle of people holding hands. I pick it up; raise it above my head pausing ever so briefly so I can see Janice's terrified face. I stare right into her eyes and I smash it to pieces in front of her on the table. Then I grab a picture off the wall, some abstract art thing. I smash it over the chair next to me. The glass shatters and flies everywhere. I can hear Janice crying and I am in a full, violent, rage. It feels so good. I grab a plant in the corner of the room by the stem. It is in a heavy floor pot so the plant comes out of the dirt. I fling that across the room dirt flying everywhere. Not satisfied I grab the floor-to-ceiling bookcase sitting on the floor and pull it forward tipping all the books onto the floor. Then I pick up the chair I was sitting in. I smash it so hard against the wall I make a hole through the drywall into the next room. Now, people are at the door, looking in through the slit of glass that runs the length of the door.

And then the verbal abuse starts pouring out of me, "Anger management, anger management, you fuckers have no idea about anger management. You have no idea what I have done, who I am! Does Charles Manson need anger management? That's a bit like putting a band aid on a hatchet wound isn't it? You stupid lesbian bitches aren't happy unless your bullying some poor fuck into doing what you want. I am out of here. Find your way to a salad bar you fat fuck of a person." And with that, I yank open the office door, I push my way past everyone and I am off to my room. I push my way past the audience and go to my room slamming the door behind me. On my bed, I feel good. I feel back in control. I feel like a weight has been lifted off of my chest. That's the problem with violence, it's self rewarding. Laying on my bed a deep sense of satisfaction comes over me. Satisfaction is what I feel, what I don't feel is guilt, remorse, compassion. In my mind Janice got what she deserved. She cornered me and I came out swinging. One of the advantages of being suicidal is you don't care what happens to you, after all I am prepared to kill myself. Anything else before that seems quite reasonable. That was just good fun. Now I feel in control.

I knew there had to be a response to the coffee pot incident. If it is not going to be a punitive response, it at least has to be therapeutic.

My curiosity has me wondering about what may happen next. Someone will come, they always do, probably Janice, maybe the police. In the end Janice comes with her supervisor, Emily. I have moved up the corporate ladder. Emily is dressed a little more business like with a pantsuit and pumps for shoes. She is wearing thick rimmed dark glasses that cover her plucked eyebrows. It has been maybe an hour since I tore up their interview room, so they have had time to meet and collect their thoughts. So have I.

I offer, "Janice, I am really sorry about the coffee pot incident and the interview room. I have this thing about being touched or cornered, when I don't expect it, I just react, violently. You don't know how many times on the street I have been robbed or groped while I was asleep. It's really affected me. It makes me crazy. I have been victimized so many times. I will never be the same. I have a solution that I would like to offer if I could. I am really starting to connect with Dr. Colby, our sessions are going well. I am really opening up. I don't want to mess that up. Can I discuss this idea of anger management with him? If he thinks it's a good idea, I will do it."

That should do it, I am thinking. A psychiatrist is a demigod in the hierarchy of helping professions. They are the top of the food chain. What they say, goes. I know I can talk Dr. Colby out of the anger management idea. He is my bitch. I am looking at Janice and it is clear I have put her in an awkward spot. She has marching orders from her colleagues. My tirade in the interview room would not diminish the idea of anger management. If she doesn't come back to the staff group, now, with me registered in anger management there may be consequences. At the same time she knows the psychiatrist rules. The consequences are real. I can tell by the look on Janice's face, there is something big on the line here. Emily is of no use. She has brought nothing to this little scenario. She is a bureaucrat in attendance as a witness. What to do?

I fish, "Janice, will you be in trouble if I don't go to anger management?"

An honest response, "Well, some of the staff are afraid for their own safety. You know, they go home, tell their husbands or partners and suddenly people are quoting labour laws and stuff. People can refuse work they think isn't safe."

Wow, I am powerful, but I need more. "Did they discuss kicking me out?"

I can tell by Janice's face the answer is yes, but she offers, "No one wants to do that."

Now we have a party. All the guests have arrived. I have divided the staff group, polarized them into camps. Here are the dynamics.

There are a group of staff who believe that I am beyond what the shelter can manage. They believe that I should be in a psychiatric facility with nurses, medications and big burly orderlies.

There is another group of staff who believe I am the perfect client for the shelter. In fact I am the poster child for the shelter. I am why the shelter was built, the perfect victim.

Now, the first group, can really be nasty. They can undermine, provoke, even set me up to fail, to prove their point, to be right.

The second group are going to kiss my ass. This will be a festival of indulgence, catering, placating and lenience. They too need to be right.

This is the type of dynamic that leads to resignations, mass exoduses from agencies.

In the middle, I don't care and therein lies my power. I have

no investment either way. I can walk out of the shelter and be fine.
I offer Janice an exit door. "Janice, why don't you or someone come to my next appointment with Dr. Colby and we can discuss the idea. If he is OK with it, I will go."

It's bit of an olive branch. I am not refusing so that should please the group ready to have me in a straight jacket. I am getting help so that should please the shelter purists.

Staring at Janice's face I can tell she isn't finished, there is more, more marching orders. With Emily present, Janice is more direct.

She begins, "I want to discuss your stay here. You have been on the street, homeless, for a long time. I think we should consider that you live here for eight months to a year and then move to second stage housing."

I am shocked. I didn't expect this. I function meal to meal, not even day to day. This proposal is a couple of years worth of planning. What would I do here for eight months to a year? That sounds more like a prison sentence than a housing arrangement.

Janice continues, "You have been here for almost a month now. You have engaged with Dr. Colby for therapy. You don't seem to be suffering from any withdrawal symptoms so I am assuming any addiction issues are under control. There is a lot you could accomplish while you are here. We can work on getting you your GED or some college certifications. It's an opportunity to make some changes."

I have had enough. I am really not sure what I want but I am not leaning towards stability. I have to blow this up. I can't be case managed like this. These people just never give up. I came to the shelter to clean up, get my bearings and move on. Now I have therapy, anger management, case management, high school credits, and second stage housing. I feel like I am being painted into a corner and I am starting to boil, again. For me this signals me to come out swinging, upset the apple cart. I am fantasizing about coming across the table at Janice and biting the nose off of her fat face but that would attract too much attention. Busting up a room is different from busting up a staff member. Interesting, how I can be in control while out of control. What is wrong with these people? Why ruin a good thing? I am good, working day to day, minding my own business. This is system-driven madness. Some bureaucrat who wouldn't recognize a client if they fell over one decided that if you are in a shelter, by thirty days in the shelter there should be a plan of care. It's a format that doesn't fit for me. I am ready to snap, again. I can feel it. This is just too intrusive, all up in my grill. I need to find a way to get them to back off but it can't be so crazy that I end up back in the hospital or out on the street. I shut down, become silent, withdrawn and then I am left alone.

The next day Janice is sitting with me in Dr. Colby's office. He is so polite, professional, restrained. I am ready to snap all over Janice. He is direct. "Janice, what can I help you with?"

Janice is well rehearsed. "Well Dr. Colby, we faxed you the incident report concerning the coffee pot incident and the interview room. We are thinking Margaret should participate in some anger management."

Dr. Colby is quick with his response. "No, Janice. Margaret has some issues beyond anger management that require psychiatric attention. Anger management is inappropriate at this time. This recommendation is akin to suggesting you wipe blood away from an open wound but not close the wound. I also hope you are not shoving case planning down Margaret's throat. You will lose her if you start on about housing contracts and second stage housing."

Well, that took the air out of the room. Janice sat quietly like she had been scolded by her father. Clearly Dr. Colby has been around the block and knows the shelter, their tactics, their agenda. He puts them in their place.

The doctor looks to send Janice on her way. "Is that it Janice? Do you need me to write that down for you, no anger management and no case management, at this time?" Janice gets up and leaves the office. With the door closed, the doctor turns to me. "Have they been giving you a hard time? They are well intentioned. They just have no idea what they are doing. I hope this hasn't set you back? I will keep them off your back as long as you are committed to your therapy. Can we pick up your story? I believe you were in the foster home being overly indulged by the foster mom."

I am in awe but at the same time a little disappointed. The doctor solved my problems at the shelter for me. I was looking forward to further terrorizing the staff with a well planned strategy of violence to get them to back off and leave me alone. The doctor put them in their place with one well spoken professional intervention. The doctor continues to impress.

The doctor has earned more of my story and I continue, "Mrs. Switzer is over the top. I have gone from poverty to wealth in less than a week. I, at that point, didn't know what to think. It was truly surreal. We have been shopping. I had never been shopping until that moment. Once back at the foster home we have an impromptu fashion show and put the clothes away in my dresser and closet. Again, until that moment I had never had either, a closet or dresser. I lived out of baskets and bags. I would often wear the same clothes, including underwear for days at a time. I may be a replacement child for Mrs. Switzer so she doesn't annoy her husband but I don't care. I am enjoying the ride. I am experiencing many new things and there are more to come."

"The next day there is another first for me. Mrs. Switzer says that it is girl time. We go to the spa and we get the works, pedicure, manicure, facial, hair, massage even aromatherapy. Mrs. Switzer is amazing, happy, joyful, full of energy, positive energy. She sees the world from a perspective I have never witnessed. Everything is possible, there are no limits, barriers, excuses. I remain suspicious, quiet, polite but reserved. It seems too good to be true and you know where that phrase goes. If it's too good to be true, it probably is."

"I am not sure how to tell you this. It's less than a week of being at the Switzer's, maybe, the fifth night. I of course am still ten years old. It's odd because I think I should have seen this coming but my radar did not go off. Mrs. Switzer's energy had me intoxicated, distracted. Anyway, it's about the fifth night that I am at their house. I am in my bed. It's amazing, clean pyjamas, sheets that smell like heaven, my head is on a pillow, a pillow! Asleep, a deep sleep, I stir, I am not alone. I feel a hand up under my pyjamas on my chest. I become aware enough to realize that it's Lucas, the Switzer's eighteen-year-old son. He has one hand on my chest and one hand on his own dick. When he realizes I am awake and he stops, it's an odd moment. Expecting violence I freeze up but he begins to talk softly to me. I had been through this nonsense with my grandfather. He was violent, forcing himself on me. Lucas tells me that he loves me and he just wants to touch me. He says he wants a special relationship with me but no one must know because if they found out, I would have to leave their home. Psychological threats seem even more powerful than physical threats. An abandoned child being threatened with abandonment is the ultimate form of control.

Quietly he pulls away from me, tucks me in, kisses my forehead and leaves my room."

"I am just a little kid. I don't have options. I have no place to go, no one to call, no one to tell. I am the perfect victim, powerless, a foster child, abandoned by parents, poor, dirty, who would believe me? Besides, I am in the safest place in the Province, foster care. The next morning at breakfast, with Mr. and Mrs. Switzer present, Lucas and I exchange some glances over orange juice and Belgian waffles. It's enough that he knows I am not going to say anything. The next day is to be my first day at the new school. My mind, my little ten-year-old brain is pretty screwed up. The affection, the tenderness Lucas showed me, made me feel good. I know that sounds screwed up, but, really, that is in my head. Today, I know different. I know that is abuse, but at the time, in my little psychology, I felt sort of special. All this of course escalated the nonsense. Lucas is persistent if nothing else, back the next night, softly talking to me, about loving me, loving having a little sister, how our relationship is special, all the while jerking off and touching my chest. I don't even have breasts, but within a week he has his finger inside me, by the end of the month I am sucking his dick. It's not every night, but it is often enough to be a routine. I am becoming aware of my own sexuality way too early and I don't have the cognitive or emotional maturity to deal with it. I am experiencing physical pleasure in this, feeling special emotionally, but also becoming aware of the power my sexuality holds. Lucas is not violent or physically threatening. He worries about me and I begin to exploit our relationship. Lucas has a job, money, resources. I begin to ask for things which hastens to demanding things and he complies with my demands."

"Then, as a reflection of my screwed up head, I get caught, fondling myself at school. Bored, without really thinking, I am masturbating in class. I sit at the back of the class, so no other kids are looking at me. Their heads are facing forward. I have my hand fully down my pants and I am fondling myself, quietly, joyfully, during geography. I wasn't confronted in class but at recess I was asked by the teacher to go to the principal's office. The last time I was in a principal's office I was being told my grandfather was dead and I was off to a foster home."

"There I am again, in the principal's office, sitting in a banker's style wooden chair. My feet don't reach the floor. There are four adults in the room with me, the principal, my teacher, the French teacher and the school nurse. Apparently, the French teacher, Miss Boudreaux, was walking the hall and peeked in through door of my classroom. She saw me with my hand down my pants. Her view of the situation did not include the word masturbation and here come the biases. I of course was the new kid, add to that the new foster kid, well really, the only foster kid. Miss Boudreaux thought I was scratching myself, because I was dirty down there, therefore the school nurse is in attendance. It was all pretty awkward but they are telling me that they want me to see a doctor, a children's doctor. The principal is on the phone to my foster mother as I wait out in the hallway. This is torture as all the children march past me coming in from recess. I already have the label of foster child, now I am sitting in front of the principal's office. The stares, the glances, the snobby, stuck-up gestures are almost intolerable. In 1970, being in front of the principal's office has a different meaning. I must be in trouble. I am the little, skinny, dirty, foster child, now with behavioural problems. That is who I am, at ten years of age and it is about to get even more interesting, more complicated."

Chapter Seven

Not All Running is Exercise

We are here on Earth to do good to others.
What the others are here for, I don't know.
– W. H. Auden

The story is progressing well with Dr. Colby. I am feeling better about getting all this mess, these memories, these feelings, that sit inside me, out. It's a purging. We are only scratching the surface. There are some really scary pieces to this story that I cannot yet tell Dr. Colby. I am always holding something back. This is one way, a strategy, to keep myself safe. No one can ever really know me. That way, when I lose them or discard them I feel no grief because we were never really attached. They never really knew me. I use people. I am using Dr. Colby. He is a means to an end. I am hiding at the shelter.

Back to the Dr.'s office for more story telling. The doctor and I have a routine now. I jump right in to continue the story. I know exactly where I left off. It's like one long story now. "After the meeting at the school I go to a family physician and then a paediatrician. I have had some medical tests. My foster mom takes me to the appointments and we are met at the paediatrician's by my Children's Aid Society social worker. I can't remember her name. There were so many. They came and went like the seasons. On this one occasion we are at the follow-up visit. I have been through a very intrusive physical exam, some tests, blood, urine, an x-ray leading up to this. This session is for feedback. The results are in and now my foster mom and social worker get to hear the diagnosis.

The doctor takes me in to an examination room and sits me on the examination table. I remember the room perfectly. It's one of those flash bulb memories, a moment you never forget, burnt into your mind. I can see even now, the examination table with the stirrups; the wax roll of never ending paper; the blood pressure cuff; the stethoscope; the jars with cotton balls, Q-tips; the plastic half heart; the little tin sink; the posters about the evils of smoking, drinking, steroids. This room is also the doctor's office with his desk, filing cabinet, pictures of his family, piles of charts. The doctor gives me a quick check. He listens to my heart, my lungs. He looks into my eyes with a small flashlight. Carefully he goes up and down my arms, squeezing, asking me if it hurts. Both my ears are peered into with another funny light. Seemingly content the doctor brings in my foster mom and social worker. They sit in chairs in front of his desk. Mrs. Switzer nervously smiles at me. The doctor pulls this white curtain around me and the examination table. I will never forget the sound of that curtain, the metal curtain rings, on the metal bar were like fingernails on a chalkboard. I am sitting there, on the exam table, staring at the white curtain. I don't know if he is delusional but he begins to talk to my foster mother and social worker, like I can't hear him."

"Here is what I hear. The doctor says, 'Thanks for coming in, I am Dr. Smith. I am afraid that we have some serious issues to discuss. I examined Margaret and ran some tests. I am not sure where to begin. Perhaps we should begin with the most serious. Margaret is sexually active. When I examined her vaginal area it was clear from bruising and colouring, that she had had sex, probably the night before. Her hymen is not intact.' There is a long pause. 'Margaret has chlamydia.' There is another long pause. 'Margaret has an anxiety disorder that has her pulling her hair out of her head.' There is a long pause. 'Margaret has tearing in her rectum, probably from anal intercourse or objects being inserted there.' There is a long pause. 'Margaret has had a broken forearm, a broken fibula and a broken scapula.' There is a long pause."

"I can't believe the doctor says all that and thinks I can't hear it sitting behind a white curtain. I had no idea what hymen meant, or chlamydia or anxiety disorder, really, but I knew it all didn't sound good. I knew life, moving forward from here, would never be the same."

"Dr. Colby, even today, I have to wonder, what conversations must have gone on from that meeting forward? I was driven back to the foster home by Mrs. Switzer. It was a quiet, long ride home. What must have been going on in her head? The paediatrician has just told her that I am having sex with someone, while I am living in her home. Perhaps she knows it is Lucas. Does she suspect her husband? Where does life go from here? I remember a quiet, silent, dinner with Mr. Switzer, Mrs. Switzer and Lucas. Had Mrs. Switzer discussed the meeting with the doctor with Mr. Switzer? It wasn't until after dinner that the reaction began. The social worker came to the foster home. I knew this was trouble because it was after dinner, after office hours. Only bad things happen after business hours. I remember sitting on my bed. The social worker, I think her name was Teresa, but that is a guess really. She is sitting across from me on my desk chair. I remember the look on her face. She was lost, out of her league, terrified. It was a worst case scenario. I am in foster care. Foster care is supposed to be part of a protection plan. I am in the foster home to keep me safe and now they have been told that someone is having sex with me. They don't know who. I am ten. My world is pretty small. I go to school and stay at the foster home. It would be better for them if it were someone at school, but not likely. Do they suspect Lucas?"

"The social worker is there to sort this mess out. I can tell she is not sure how to ask me who is boning me but it does spill awkwardly out of her. It goes something like this, 'Margaret, the doctor is suggesting that someone is sexually abusing you. He is saying, without a doubt, this is happening. It's not a maybe or a possibility. He is saying, absolutely, without doubt, someone is sexually abusing you. Is someone touching you in your private area?'"

"I may only be ten but I know the answer to that question is going to blow up my foster home. I am also pretty sure that when push comes to shove, the Switzers are going to pick their son, Lucas, over me. I will be out of the foster home. I knew this home, this family was too good to be true."

"The social worker puts on the pressure with, 'Margaret, we need to know so we can protect you. If you don't tell me, I am going to have to remove you from the Switzer's to insure your protection. It means another foster home.'"

"I did not expect that, a move, another foster home, another family. Once that was spoken, a panic came over me. I had been through so much disruption already. It would be an understatement to say I was scared and confused. Should I tell on Lucas? Should I lie and make a false accusation against someone outside the Switzer home? Should I just say nothing and see what happens? Dr. Colby, it was at this moment that I learned about the power of being a victim. It became abundantly clear, even in my ten-year-old little head, that my words were going to generate tremendous influence and change. In the end, in this circumstance, I decided to say nothing. I had no anger towards Lucas. I did not feel he was abusing me, exploiting me or victimizing me. I was sort of participating. There was no agenda to hurt Lucas or see him in trouble. Vulnerable to the attention, the affection, I was emotionally seduced into an odd compliance. At some level I understood what was happening to be wrong, because it involved secrets and emotional pressure, yet someone was making me feel special."

"In the end, in my silence, the social worker packs up my new clothes and walks me out of the Switzer's home. There were no goodbyes, no hugs, no best wishes, with the Switzers. I climb into the social worker's car and we quietly drive away. I have no idea where I am going, what will be next, where I will live. There is no closure with the Switzers. I still to this day have no idea what happened to them as a family. I never told anyone, until you, Dr. Colby, what happened with Lucas. Here, some thirty- six years later, it matters very little to me. I have lived enough experiences for five lifetimes. What happened between Lucas and me, to me, today, is of no significance. It does not sit as a huge unresolved issue. I suppose from one perspective, I was sexually abused by Lucas. I just don't see it that way."

Chapter Eight

Even the Hippies Became the Yuppies

One thing I can tell you is you've got to be FREE!
– John Lennon

I am surprised how well the sessions with Dr. Colby are going. He is compassionately listening without judging me. The story is flowing easily. My recall is surprisingly clear, accurate, despite all the substance abuse and hard living, my memory is good. Once again, back in Dr. Colby's office, in another session, I am moving the story forward. I think the doctor hoped the story had reached a climax, not so. This story is a long, slow boil. Back in my comfortable chair in the doctor's soft office I continue the tale.

"The social worker removes me from the Switzer's home without goodbyes. She drives for miles, it's late, and we arrive at another home, an emergency intake foster home. I have no idea where I am. The introductions are short and sweet because of the late hour. I am shuffled off to a bedroom and put to bed. In the dark, I can see that I have a roommate but I am exhausted and I go to sleep. It is a restless, fitful sleep of dreams and night terrors."

"In the morning I am awakened by the foster mom. I see my roommate is a girl who looks a few years older than I am. The foster mom is a character. She looks like she enjoyed the sixties way too much. She was a hippy, a true flower child. She had long brown greying hair down to the middle of her back, the most welcoming brown eyes, no makeup and she wore a red bandana straight from Jimmy Hendrix. Her tie-dyed shirt hung open as she bent down to rub my hair and I could see her peace symbol tattoo on her breast. Her glasses had perfectly round slightly blue-coloured lenses. Her bell bottom jeans fit her slim body perfectly. In her bare feet she looked like she came straight from Haight-Ashbury. As she led us to the kitchen for breakfast she told me to call her Candy. My roommate's name is Carolyn, Carolyn Skye. In the kitchen there are four more children of various ages, seated at the large harvest table. It's pretty quiet with Captain Crunch cereal, toast and orange juice. The house is an amazing century-old farm house with a dumb waiter, fire places in every room, huge sliding pocket doors and a wrap-around porch. There are seven bedrooms, three bathrooms, two living rooms and a massive basement. After breakfast Candy gives me a tour of the whole house. It is clear this is Candy's little piece of heaven. She loves her home and she loves her job of foster mother. She has room enough for ten children."

"I am back in my room with my new roommate, Carolyn. She tells me that she is fifteen and has been in this intake home for six weeks while Children's Aid Society looks for a permanent home for her. I hear the sadness in her voice. She tells me we are in Allentown. Allentown is the city closest to Ivan where my grandfather's trailer sat. Allentown is also where my mother lives, I think. Allentown is about an hour away from Toronto. I am home in a sense."

"We are alone in our room, Carolyn and I, swapping stories about how we came to be in care. Our stories are eerily similar. Carolyn's father is nowhere to be found. Carolyn's mother makes very poor choices in men. Carolyn has been beaten by her mother and is now in foster care for the third time. Carolyn, in her orientation of me to herself, introduces me to a new behaviour, a new concept, running. Carolyn is a runner. She runs away and she is about to leave the hippy foster home. Carolyn explains that she has a place to stay downtown where we will be cared for. Carolyn wants me to come with her and with just that much, we run. There was no real planning or preparation. We just stepped out the front door and left. I haven't been in the hippy home for twelve hours and I am on the run with Carolyn, a fifteen year old that I have known for a couple of hours. Shortly, I am in downtown Allentown with Carolyn. She is holding my hand, leading me I don't know where, but we are on the run. I am Carolyn's apprentice, her protégé."

"Allentown is a city of one hundred and twenty thousand people. It has all the scary things a city of that size should have, drugs, prostitution, gangs. Surprisingly, Carolyn knows exactly where she is going. She says it is a safe house and we will be looked after there, fed. The house isn't a house at all. It is a ratty, filthy apartment above a boarded-up store in an ugly part of downtown. The area looks more like a bombed-out section of Beirut than a downtown in an Ontario city. There are mattresses on the floor, blankets over the windows, a broken couch full of holes, garbage everywhere. There are no lights, electricity. It is, at best, a squatters shit-hole. The smell reminds me of the trailer. "

"And then there are the people. Initially I counted eight peo-

ple in this one-bedroom slum. There are three men, four women and one child. Drugs, out of control, pot, acid, heroin, you name it, there it was, out in the open. This was a sixties scene gone bad. These people came together in love and peace and arrived at addiction and poverty. I am still feeling relatively neutral about being in this place. There is no fear, no intimidation. It is at some level still peace and love. Carolyn introduces me to Jake. Jake is the leader of this little mob. He hugs Carolyn and asks,
'Were you at the Hippy's?'
Carolyn responds, 'Yes, Jake, mom had me pinned at home. I couldn't get out and then the CAS appeared.'
Jake comforts her, 'It's OK Carrie. It happens, welcome home, you OK to work?' Jake is staring at me, very intently, too intently. It is making me uncomfortable.
Carolyn responds with, 'Sure Jake.'"
"We eat sandwiches and play cards, crazy eights, and then we go out. Jake, Carolyn and I begin to walk around downtown Allentown. We settle into the entrance of a store. Jake is chain smoking cigarettes. Carolyn is looking up and down the street. I have no idea what is going on. Then, a car stops at the curb, in front of us. Jake approaches the car, words are exchanged that I cannot hear. Jake comes back and Carolyn goes and gets in the car."
"Jake says to me, 'He's cool, I know him from before, we'll wait here.'"
"I am lost in a naive fog, standing in the doorway, oblivious, with Jake. Jake is drug abuse skinny, covered in tattoos. Even his face has tattoo markings, his arms, neck all inked up. He is not scary looking or abrupt in his language. He seems cool in his denim vest, black T-shirt, jeans and sandals. He looks like he is in his thirties. Maybe ten minutes went by and the same car pulled up and Carolyn jumped out. She was smiling and handed Jake some money. Jake hugs her and tells her she has done well."
"Back at the apartment we have pizza. There is laughter, stories, connection, even love. After we eat, Jake sits with me, Carolyn is also there. He begins to talk softly to me. He says, 'Margaret, Maggie, my little one, this is our family. We live together, work together, survive together. We help one another, everyone contributes, everyone plays a role, does their part. You are welcome to stay here with no strings attached. We won't pressure you into anything

you don't want to do but you have to help out. Are you with me Maggie? Two things you get today from your new family. You get a nickname and a tattoo. The family picks both. I love you Maggie."

"The family comes and forms a circle by sitting on the floor around me. They hold hands and sort of hum. Suddenly, one of the women looks at me and says, 'Skully.' There is a little more humming and one of the men says, 'Spider.' As I sit there, Jake tattoos a spider on my hand at the base of my thumb. I have been initiated into the family."

"Dr. Colby? This is a three-year story all by itself. Do you want me to tell the whole story? I am ten going on eleven and I am living in this drug-infested, corrupt world they call a family. I am introduced to prostitution, drug running, drug pushing, theft, scams and more criminal behaviour."

Dr. Colby responds, "You were involved in prostitution?"

I, in a matter-of-fact manner respond, "Yes." I can tell the doctor's curiosity is beyond professional. He wants to know how a ten-year-old girl finds her way to prostitution.

I add, "Dr. Colby, it took me a long time to figure some of this underworld out, this family. Nothing is ever what it seems. It looks like one thing but really it's another. Here is a twist for you, an example. Carolyn, the fifteen year old that I met at the Hippy's, was a recruiter. She was sent, by Jake, to get me, to find me. I mean, not me specifically but someone like me. Carolyn was Jake's prize. He had complete control over her. Jake sent Carolyn back to her mother, called Children's Aid Society and orchestrated her placement at the Hippy's. None of that was random. He knew the system, intimately, how it worked. He grew up in it. Carolyn waited for six weeks at the Hippy's for me to arrive. Twenty kids must have gone through that home before I got there. In her mind I was the perfect mark she was looking for, young, naive, completely homeless, vulnerable. She had me pegged within minutes of my arrival. The predators of the world can spot a victim, prey, a mile away. I was ripe for the picking. The family is playing me, playing to my vulnerability, my need to belong, to feel loved. Once they had me, they anointed me, initiated me and then turned me out to the streets. It's a seduction, an abrupt indoctrination, a brainwashing."

The doctor seems shocked. He answers, "I think you should tell this part of the story, Margaret. The world you grew up in is, not the real world. At ten you are in the prime of your moral development. To be exposed to these things, prostitution, drugs, crime, at ten, it's going to twist your development into a knot. You really don't stand a chance for a healthy development in that environment. I believe it would help to have the story told."

I agree, but in my head a worry develops. Dr. Colby is bright, but how bright? He knows I am screwed up, but can he guess or figure out, just how screwed up I really am?

Chapter Nine

Hope, Dope & How to Cope

Walking back to the shelter from Dr. Colby's office I feel a little better. This therapy may actually be working, helping. There is a jump in my step, an energy I haven't felt for a while. A feeling that I have not experienced in a long time floats around me—hope.

Then as I turn the last corner to the shelter a panic grips me. It is all so fragile. There are four police squad cars with lights flashing in front of the shelter. I can also see an ambulance, a fire truck and a television news van. This is rare for the shelter and it can only mean trouble, for someone. I try to talk myself out of the panic. I am rationalizing that they are not there for me but as I approach with my business as usual gait, a young officer begins to walk towards me. I feel a psychological rip tide go through my entire body, a tsunami of fear. This can't be good. My heart is pounding out of my chest. My thoughts are racing. There are so many reasons that I should be bent over a squad car in hand cuffs. I can't hide in innocence. For a moment I consider running, bolting to safety, but I can't see a gun, or pepper spray, or tazer or even hand cuffs being presented so I steer the course.

The officer now only a few feet away from me says, "Are you Margaret Sellars?" Once your last name is in the equation, you know it is serious trouble. He continues, "Can we move across the street and talk, please ma'am?"

"Sure," I offer. "What is going on?"

I can tell the officer is holding back laughter. His hand keeps coming up to his face, covering his mouth. His square jaw is twitching and he replies, "I am Constable Kane, there has been an incident at the shelter. Well, a man, a husband, an angry husband, showed up today at the shelter, dressed as a woman and managed to get himself admitted to the shelter. Once in the kitchen of the shelter, he stabbed his estranged wife to death, in front of pretty much everyone. You are the only unaccounted for resident. You were out seeing your psychiatrist? It's a real mess in there and it is a crime scene, so you can't go in there just now. I know I shouldn't be laughing. It's not funny, well it's sort of funny. The husband remains at large, missing. He ran off in a dress and high heels. We don't think anyone else is at risk, at this time, but we have moved everyone out of the shelter to a community centre a few blocks from here. We expect to return everyone before night fall, but they are at the community centre, being fed, and interviewed for statements. You will also have to be interviewed. I can drive you there if you like?"

Remaining a little shocked, I reply, "Sure, Constable Kane. Thank you."

I have never been in the front seat of a police car so this is novel. This young Constable Kane has a real sense of ha ha and is giggling to himself as we drive to the community centre. He periodically breaks out in a real belly laugh, then catches himself. I can tell he is fantasizing about how a guy gets up in the morning and decides to dress up as a woman to gain entry to the shelter to kill his wife. I know he is working on his routine, rehearsing, for his friends and family as to how to best tell this story for the greatest impact. This is way better than writing speeding tickets or running the RIDE program. He must be thinking that the shelter staff are pretty stupid not to recognize a guy dressed up as a woman. There should be some dead giveaways, like facial hair, a deep voice, an oversized adams apple, grizzly large hands. Getting into the shelter is really quite difficult, even for a woman. The location is top secret so you have to get past that hurdle. Then, the door is locked, severely locked, bolted shut. There is an intercom and a camera at the entrance.

Even I am trying to visualize a guy, dressed as a woman, disguising his voice to gain entry into the shelter. Still inside the front door, you are not actually in the shelter. There is another layer of security, a door that is buzzed open from the receptionist's office to get into the common areas of the shelter. It's all so tragic and bizarre at the same time.

In my narcissistic little mind, my take on the situation, I am feeling grateful for all this because it takes the spotlight off of me. This crazed lunatic has done me a great service. I feel envy. I feel cracked. I should thank him. I may not be the number one case at the weekly case management meeting this time. This is perfect,

I am back under the radar, where I belong, where I can operate, where Skully thrives.

The scene inside the community centre is nothing short of a picture from a disaster movie. It is complete chaos. There are people crying, uncontrollably. Others are comforting them but also crying. I can't tell who are the staff and who are the residents. It's one big wailing wall.

This is the worst case scenario for the shelter, not only the shelter, but the shelter movement. The shelters are built to keep women safe. To have this violation, this penetration, threatens the integrity and strength of the whole system. Whenever there is loss, there is blame and heads are going to roll. As I walk deeper into the community centre Janice, my primary worker spots me and moves towards me. It is clear that she has been crying, and crying. Her large round face is further swollen with grief. She knows better than to touch me or hug me in any way, but she has an obligation to deal with me as my primary worker. The shelter disaster plan is in full operation. I am not reacting in sympathy with the movement or situation. No crying for me. My emotions don't match the circumstances. Someone has died, killed brutally by her estranged husband. That should generate some sadness or anger in me, but no, I feel disgust.

In my head, I need to explain this even if only for myself and Skully. I turn and walk away from Janice. I don't see her reaction to my rude behaviour. Seeing a chair near the auditorium stage I sit by myself and reflect on this whole messy dynamic hoping to have some clarity for my next session with Dr. Colby.

So, I am thinking, I don't agree with the whole victim–perpetrator view of the world. It's too easy, too convenient. The world is never that simple, that black and white, but it is a view intensely guarded by those in the shelter movement. It shows up in statements like, 'don't blame the victim'. I think it is a load of hog wash, bullshit. The rhetoric says that violence is a choice, well so is staying with a guy who is abusive, walk away. Women can be just as nasty, violent, abusive as any man. I am living proof of that. There is no such thing as gender bias in my mind.

As I wash these thoughts through my mind I see a police officer approaching me. It is the same young Constable Kane who giggled his way over here with me. He has come to take my statement.

The grin still solidly on his face he says, "Ma'am, can we talk now? Let's go to the front of the community centre, there's an office there."

Once in the office I see that there is a thick file on the desk with my name on it. The young uniformed officer takes out his note pad, sits behind the metal desk, removes his hat and asks me to recount my day.

I begin, "Our days are pretty routine at the shelter. They follow a schedule to keep everyone moving in some direction. We wake up at 8:00 every day. There is a half hour to shower, make up our rooms and get to breakfast for 8:30. We eat together in a large kitchen and then clean up after ourselves. This is all done by 9:30. My appointments with Dr. Colby are at 10:00, so today, like every Tuesday, I leave the shelter, after clean up and walk to his office. Our appointments are an hour long. When the appointments are over, we return to the shelter. That's it, nothing extraordinary."

The officer, Constable Kane, according to his name tag, looks perplexed. He asks, "Did you see anyone unusual hanging around the shelter, as you left this morning? I ask, because you were the only one outside the shelter, just before this happened."

Reflecting, searching my memory, I reply, "No."

Officer Kane opens my file and silently reviews something of the contents. He seems a little lost. He is not a detective but he has been given an assignment, orders, to do something. He continues, "Margaret, I have to ask this. Did you have anything to do with this? Our investigation is just beginning but we have learned that you have had two violent incidents in the shelter, you have a criminal record for assault causing bodily harm, you were the only one conveniently not in the shelter when this happened. There is a theory that you helped Mr. Kraus. I am sorry to say that so abruptly but we have to follow up all possibilities."

Choking back my anger I respond, "Officer Kane, in response to your first question, again, I saw no one as I left the shelter this morning. As for your 'theory', I don't know a Mr. Kraus and at this moment I don't even know who was killed at the shelter. I am in the shelter because I am homeless and I have been a victim of spousal abuse. I mind my own business. I don't know the names of any of the other residents. I have no beef with any residents."

And at that moment, almost mid-sentence, the flip, the stress of the moment, the fear, changes my demure. Now, I am Skully. Margaret is gone.

Officer Kane closes my file. "Yet you smashed one resident in the head with a coffee pot sending her to the hospital. That sounds like a beef to me. Margaret, there is more in your file here than your arrest record. You have been implicated in other crimes, suspected of things, horrible things, dating back to your grandfather's death. You were the last one to see him alive."

My self control, is out of control. It is time for me to go. My flight response is in overdrive. I say to Officer Kane, "That's a pretty wild theory. I was ten years old when my grandfather passed. Are we done here?"

"Yes, Margaret, for now, we are done. I am asking you not to leave the shelter until I say it's OK. Do we understand one another?" With that Officer Kane gets up and leaves the room.

The terror that gripped me is gone. I am calm, at peace, resolved, intent. Skully is in full control now. This day has been twisted into a knot. It started so well with Dr. Colby and the possibility of becoming even more anonymous. Now it seems I am in the cross hairs of a police investigation. If they had anything solid I would have been downtown with a detective, not in a community centre with a giggling rookie cop. I am blaming Janice. She has case managed me into being a suspect in a murder. I wouldn't mind if I had actually done it, but no, this one is not mine.

I can't ride out the shelter's disaster plan at the community centre. I decline the critical incident response debriefing therapist while enjoying the pizza and Diet Pepsi. I have never seen all the staff in one place at one time. It's all hands on deck from the executive director to the janitor, everyone is pitching in. I am looking for Janice. She is going to pay.

From the office next door I can hear Our Lady Peace,

'I walked around my good intentions
And found that there were none
I blame my father for the wasted years
We hardly talked
I never thought I would forget this hate
Then a phone call made me realize I'm wrong

And If I don't make it known that
I've loved you all along
Just like sunny days that
We ignore because
We're all dumb and jaded
And I hope to God I figure out
what's wrong

I walked around my room
Not thinking
Just sinking in this box
I blame myself for being too much
Like somebody else
I never thought I would just
Bend this way
Then a phone call made me realize I'm wrong

And if I don't make it known that
I've loved you all along
Just like sunny days that
We ignore because
We're all dumb and jaded
And I hope to God I figure out
what's wrong
And I hope to God I figure out
what's wrong
Hope to God I figure out
I hope to God I figure out
what's wrong
If I don't make it known that
I've loved you all along
Just like sunny days that
We ignore because
We're all dumb and jaded
And I hope to God I figure out
what's wrong

And If I don't make it known that
I've loved you all along'

Skully always carries a knife. It's an old habit. Strapped to her leg is a military style blade in a leather sheath. I am looking for Janice. This is the perfect predatory hunting ground, crisis, chaos, systems displaced. Janice is of course near the food eating her distress. I approach her. She sees me and I see her vulnerability. I quietly say, "Can we find a quiet place to talk?"

Janice, desperate to hear these words, says, "Of course, Margaret."

I lead Janice to a door at the rear of the auditorium that leads outside. She steps outside ahead of me as I reach for my knife. I am right behind her, scouting out the area. We are behind the community centre. It is secluded, private. As I hear the fire door close behind me I reach around Janice with my knife and slit her throat, hard. She falls face first, limp to the ground. I can see the gaping wound and know she is dying, bleeding out. She can't speak. I have cut her vocal cords, through to her spine. Air is leaking out of her. It is a very unique sound. I bend over her. I want to see her life leave her eyes. This is the thrill for me. I clean my blade on her flower coloured dress as she expires. It's beautiful. I turn putting my knife back in its sheath, pulling my jeans over the weapon. I walk around the community centre and re-enter from the front door. Returning to my chair Skully feels a tremendous sense of satisfaction. Skully has terminated that overbearing bully of a lesbian by cutting her head off. I blame her for sending the police into my world, my business. That is just not acceptable.

Soon we are allowed back into the shelter. It is late evening, the investigation is over, the crime scene tape gone. I am drawn to the kitchen. Standing in the middle of the room I imagine the crossdressing lunatic husband stabbing his estranged wife to death. I can see his wild eyes with mascara, his awkwardly drawn eyebrows, oversized lipstick and wig. It's beautiful. It has turned out to be a great day.

Chapter Ten

Relief by Definition is Temporary

Dr. Colby begins our next session. He of course has heard about the tragedy at the shelter. Not all the details are in his possession. He says, in a worrisome manner, "Margaret, lucky perhaps for you, you were with me when the tragedy occurred at the shelter. Thank God you didn't have to witness such a horrific scene. Do you wish to discuss the incident or continue your story?"

I respond, "It has been helpful unloading some of these old life events. I have felt better after our sessions, but it is only temporary. Life seems to have a way of beating me up. I can't escape my history, my past, it seems to catch up to me."

The doctor offers, "This is a long process Margaret. There is no quick fix. What happens to you after you leave here?"

I pause and reflect. Should I be honest? I decide to peel the onion one layer further for the doctor without disclosing any real details. I offer, "Back in that trailer, on the floor, with my grandfather standing over me, I developed a skill. I developed a way to separate myself from myself, to disappear, as a way to cope. Then, when bad things happened, they weren't really happening to me. Over time this skill became more refined, almost happening without any effort on my part. She, this other person that lives inside me, has a name. Her name is Skully. Skully is my alter ego. She is my champion, my protector, my warrior. When I am stressed, afraid, threatened, I become Skully. Margaret is a quiet, thinking, artististic person who wants to do well but is afraid. Skully is a loud, fearless, offensive person that has no feeling, compassion. It's like I am two people, Margaret and Skully. I can talk to Skully and she talks to me. She is my friend, the one, the only one that I can count on. Skully has been my constant, the one person I can rely on."

For the first time in our sessions Dr. Colby interrupts me. "Margaret, given what you have experienced in life this is not surprising. You are right, this is a coping mechanism. It has allowed you to survive, to compartmentalize the horror you have endured. To some degree we all possess this ability. At one level it is a form of self hypnosis, but at another level it is multiple personality disorder. Multiple personality disorder can be a serious condition where one acts out of character, inside another moral code. I suggest you continue your story and we will try to identify when Skully appears. OK?"

I agree with this, "I am not sure where I left off."

The doctor reminds me. "You had been initiated into a seedy little hippy group."

I pick up the trail. "That's right, I ran from the foster home with Carolyn, Carrie. She was fifteen and prostituting under the control of Jake, her pimp. I was vulnerable, homeless with no family. Jake started me with being a mule for drugs. That was my job in the family. I was turning eleven and transporting drugs around the city, even across the border from the United States to Canada. I am good at this, innocent, with ten pounds of cocaine strapped to my body. A woman in the group, Elaine, acts as my mom and we go back and forth across the border a couple of times a month. We are a team."

I prefer to move pot. We buy it and sell it. The people around pot are friendly, quiet, placid, high. The people around cocaine are scary, jittery, there are always guns, paranoia. I am eleven or twelve years old in meetings with machine guns, bags of money, in alleys, vacant lots and basements."

"At twelve years old, Dr. Colby, I kill someone. It's a drug deal gone bad. I don't even know how many people were there, in the dark. We are in an old warehouse of some kind. They had maybe, five people, we had four. It's always really tense. We are there for the exchange. We are selling the cocaine I had just muled in from the U.S. Jake is counting the money and the money is short and all hell breaks loose. Shooting, screaming, running, bullets flying everywhere and then there is me, or Skully, ducking for cover. Jake has shot two people. They are dead. Two have run off. One remains alive. He is wounded. Shot in the leg. He is a black man, wearing a biker's vest, colours. He is there for muscle, hired help. We don't deal with bikers as a rule. Jake is standing over him, furious about the money being short. Jake calls me over, there is a long pause as we stare at the biker. I sense what Jake wants me to do. He hands me the gun and tells me to shoot him, in the head. The gun is heavy, really heavy. It takes both my hands to hold the gun. Skully steadies the weapon, points it straight at the head of the biker and pulls the trigger. There is a loud bang, really loud, deafening. The recoil on the gun knocks me on my ass. The biker's head explodes like a watermelon dropped from a building. He shakes, tremors really and then goes still. He is dead. Jake says he is proud of me, that this an important step for me in the family. Skully has killed a man."

"Back at the apartment, Jake tells the story like it's a wild west shoot out. He is so excited. We have the cocaine and the money, even if it is short. He tells the group that I shot and killed a biker, with such pride, smiling, patting me on my little bald head. He is talking like I am his daughter scoring her first goal at a soccer game. Jake pretends to be me, struggling to hold up the gun then falling on my butt after pulling the trigger. The group cheers for me. We party all night. I am twelve years old and I have already killed two people. It seems surreal, impossible. I haven't even reached puberty and I have killed two people. I have killed two people and gotten away with it. The police don't put a lot of investigative effort into a dead biker. I feel, I feel, empowered, omnipotent, detached. Killing is somewhere inside my moral code now as an acceptable behaviour. I feel that I have the right to kill. The world has been evil to me. I am just a little kid. I didn't ask to be born. I have never felt safe, secure, like there are things, people that I can trust, that someone has my back, is looking out for me. I have been starved, beaten, sexually abused, degraded, told I am worthless, a waste of good sperm. Now, I feel it is my turn. The victim becomes the perpetrator."

The doctor, Doctor Colby, looks like a deer in the head lights. He is bound by confidentiality. He can't rat me out, besides it's over thirty years ago. I am waiting for a reaction. We sit in silence for a full ten minutes. We are in the filth of my life, the full stench of my existence, the stark reality of the horror that is my life. The doctor seems lost. Finally in a broken sentence he says, "Can you continue Margaret?"

I am not sure where to go with recounting this part of my life but I continue. "Carolyn is my mentor. She is grooming me, caring for me. In the apartment she teaches me things. As a gift, she gives me a military style knife and a leather sheath. She has the same knife. It is beautiful with a sharp curved blade, a serrated edge, a moulded grip and brown leather sheath. Carrie teaches me how to strap the sheath to my ankle and hide it under my pant leg. We practice, for hours pulling it out, brandishing it, like a gunslinger with a six shooter. Carrie tells me that 'Johns' are sometimes violent. Rehearsing, pretending we are sitting in the front seat of a car, side by side, we take turns. Carrie pretends to be the John, I am leaning over like I am giving oral sex. Carrie grabs my hair and I pull out the knife and stab, first in the leg, then the stomach. Then we reverse roles. Carrie has the same knife but greater skills. These are important survival skills."

"Carrie teaches me how to give good head, with a banana. She shows me how to hide a condom under my tongue and slip it on a penis without the John even knowing. Carrie demonstrates how to cradle a man's balls, to stroke the shaft and then to maximize pleasure gently twist the testicles at the moment of ejaculation. It's a game, but, at the same time, I being trained, groomed. Carrie tells me that there are men that have fetishes and a little girl like me can make a lot of money. I still don't have a concept of money. Carrie is like an older sister, showing me the ropes, helping me find my way in this new environment. She has an obvious affection for me. Carrie brushes my hair, teaches me about makeup and helps me buy clothes. She is looking out for me. "

Dr. Colby again seems transfixed, uncomfortable. I pause and he does not interject. I see that our time is up, I get up and leave the office.

Chapter Eleven

Kaboom!

We can never obtain peace in the
outer world until
we make peace with ourselves.
– Dalai Lama

Returning, the shelter seems to have a collective emotional concussion. Everyone remains in shock. It is very quiet, sombre. People are returning to their normal routine but the energy level is quite different. Being that close to two murders gives people a different perspective on life. The Urgent Memorandum pinned to the wall in the common kitchen contains the words, 'The tragic murder of a resident has been followed by the killing of one of our own staff, Janice Albright …'.

The rumours in the shelter are rampant. I hear the whispers. The theory is that the same person killed both people. This theory is projected further to the belief that the shelter has been targeted and remains at risk. There is a high security alert, with additional staff present. They have hired a private security business, with female security guards. They are both inside and outside the shelter doing regular rounds and checks. I wonder if they too believe I am a player in this conspiracy. They don't seem to be following me or giving me any special attention. The police certainly had me placed somewhere near the murder of the resident. They suggested to me that I helped him. The police have not been back to me, to ask questions, since the murders. The shelter seems content to have me live there and attend my appointments with Dr. Colby, yet I sense something else is going on behind the scenes. It still bounces through my head that I should move on, run, but I don't act on these powerful impulses. There is something about these dynamics that keeps me stationary and fascinated at the same time.

I am shocked at the lack of response on the part of the shelter, both staff and residents, towards me. If I am a suspect of some kind, any kind, this should generate some attention. I would think they would be all over me for answers to resolve this in their own minds. Am I a risk? Are they researching me to confront me? It is all so intriguing to see if I can outsmart them all.

Finally, there is some action. The shelter's executive director wants to meet with me, another step up the corporate ladder. She comes to my room and asks me to come to her office. I have never met or even seen her before. The executive director never operates alone. She is a shadow moving with other shadows. She wants lots of witnesses. I have not seen her interact with shelter residents. She is an evil administrator, getting funding, managing risk exposure, hiring staff, strategic planning. If she wants to talk to me I have become a liability to the shelter, no more Mr. Nice Guy.

We enter her disaster of an office. There are four other people waiting there, in attendance at our unscheduled meeting. If they have five people in attendance, this is not a meeting, it is a plot. I don't recognize any of the other people as staff of the shelter. Reading the dress and presentation I surmise that one is a lawyer, uptight, never had an orgasm, bitch. The notepad paper is a dead give away. Two of them appear to be board members. They are dressed in business wear but seem out of place somehow. The other one is clutching a very large briefcase. I assume they are from the local Ministry Office where the shelter gets its money. I peg no one as a cop. Although it seems I am legally safe, my quick assessment of the situation is that I am in deep shit.

I am a person of the street, with street smarts. I am a gypsy. Reading people is one of my many talents. I am an expert at interpreting micro reflexes, those small eye movements, posture, head positioning, the eyebrows, all tell a story. My gut reaction, as I enter the executive director's office and sit with this distinguished group of people is that I am going to be asked to leave the shelter. The lawyer is necessary because I do have rights. I am essentially a tenant at the shelter. They are going to twist my rights into a weapon and stab me with them. Sitting down my anxiety is escalating and I am calling on Skully.

The office is a mess of paper, files, banker's boxes and office supplies. You can't see the top of the executive director's desk. The shelter is built into a hill, so the back of the building, where we are, is at grade level, a walk out basement essentially.

Seated, introductions begin and suddenly there is the loudest sound I have ever heard. It is an explosion, a huge explosion. The window in the office shatters, blown out. The power of the blast knocks us all to the floor. There are things flying everywhere, parts of chairs, desks, paper, drywall, bricks, wood splinters. Suddenly I can see the sky. The women's shelter has been blown up. I am doing the self check. My ears are ringing and I can't really hear. I can't find any external physical injuries. Laying on the floor it appears I am intact. Motionless I am trying to sense any internal damage giving my body time to sense pain. Moving to stand up I feel dizzy, probably a concussion. Getting my bearings I am looking for the others, that only a moment ago, were in the room with me seated around a meeting table. The executive director is on the floor. I can hear her moaning. One of the ladies, the lawyer, has a table leg sticking out of her chest. She is motionless, eyes open, expired. Another of our meeting participants is pinned against what is left of the wall by a book shelf, not moving. She too appears to have passed. I am up, mobile, but slow, carefully checking the status of the room. The fourth lady is missing, completely. I can see fire, burning down the hall, probably the gas line. I see no other people or movement. Returning to the executive director she is asking for help, struggling. I approach her. She is reaching out, her hand trembling, asking for help. Slowly, I bend down beside her and pull out my knife. The executive director's eyes bulge out of her head, she does not have enough breath to scream out. I see another heavy table leg loose on the floor. Putting away my knife I pick up the table leg, feeling the weight of the lathed wood in my hand. It is heavy, solid, like a baseball bat. Funny how things can change so quickly, only moments ago the arrogant executive director and her posse of minions was going to toss me out on the street. Now, she needs my help. Holding the table leg above my head, I bring it down, solidly on the cranium of the executive director. It sticks in her melon of a head. There is no blood spatter. It breaks into her skull and remains embedded there. The executive director dies there in her own office. Someone should call the Health and Safety Committee.

That's enough for me, I am moving towards the daylight, now shining through where there was once a ceiling, roof, stepping through the rubble. The office has an outside wall facing the back of the building. I step through the broken window into the back patio area. As I turn around, I see that the roof of the building has been torn off. The explosion is massive damaging each building on either side of the shelter too. I walk along the side of the building towards the street. It is a struggle with bricks, wood, furniture, everywhere. Sirens are audible in the distance moving towards the shelter. As I reach the front of the building it becomes clear what has happened. Someone, I assume an angry husband, probably the angry husband, has driven their vehicle, a truck, a bomb, into the front of the shelter. My position at the moment of the blast, being at the back of the building, below grade, in the executive director's office, saved my life. The one time being in trouble actually saved my bacon. The driver of the truck has blown up himself and the shelter, ruining a perfectly good truck in the process. I walk away.

Down the street I confirm in my head that nothing good can come from remaining at the shelter under these circumstances. I have dodged enough bullets for today. It is time to move on. My disaster planning is in full effect, walk away, leave. This is how I cope best, a pure flight response. Later, on the radio at the Salvation Army Church, I hear there are seventeen dead and twelve injured from the blast. The angry husband built himself an Oklahoma City style bomb, drove his truck bomb into the front room of the shelter detonating the suicide, death by shelter weapon.

Chapter Twelve

The Horror of Life

An insincere and evil friend is more to be feared than a wild beast; a wild beast may wound your body, but an evil friend will wound your mind.
– Buddha

Showing up for my next appointment with Dr. Colby I am not sure what to expect. At the sliding glass window his secretary confirms that he is expecting me. Sitting in the soft, quiet waiting room I look at the other patients waiting. Dr. Colby is in practice with three other psychiatrists. They share office space, secretaries and dirty stories. Three other people are waiting. As I look at them I wonder what their problems might be? Are they as screwed up as I am?

As I enter Dr. Colby's office he has this intense look of relief on his face. He jumps up from behind his large oak desk and for a moment I thought he wanted to hug me but his professionalism caught him. He gestures for me to sit down and he begins, "Thank God you are OK. This is the worst tragedy I have ever experienced. The absolute horror of it is overwhelming. The shelter is gone, building, staff, everything. I am operating on the assumption that you are welcome to continue here with me. I will sort out the details of that. It's not your worry. It's mine."

I respond, "Dr. Colby? Do they, whoever they are, need to know that I am continuing to come to see you? I would rather they didn't know, if that is possible."

Dr. Colby says, "No problem. I bill them based on a number, not a name. You are entitled to confidentiality. Why?"

I offer, "I need to separate myself from the shelter. That was just all too much, two murders, a bombing. I need out of that mess with some distance."

He reassures me, "No problem. I understand completely. Once again I have to ask you what you would like to address in our session today? I trust you have housing, a place to stay?"

Respectfully I offer, "Yes, I am fine. I would like to pick up my story where we left off, if we could."

I take a sip of water and begin. "The hippy group becomes more sophisticated. They are generating some serious money and our lifestyle improves. The lights are on, electricity, running water, beds, appliances, real food from a grocery store. I find my way to video games, the original Pong. I am twelve going on thirteen, discovering clothes, shopping, makeup and the value of money. I see Carolyn making her own money and spending it on herself. Jake offers, he does not insist, to further my training in prostitution. He never forced himself on me. I begin to have sex with Jake. He instructs me on how to please a man and I begin turning tricks. Initially it's street prostitution, oral sex in cars, but I quickly develop a base of return customers. This leads to seedy motels, intercourse, and more of a call girl clientele or escort service if you will. Jake is turning me out for entire nights, even weekends. I am getting 30 percent of the take and loading up on cash. I am thirteen going on thirty, my development accelerated, shot out of a gun really. I have all the power, authority, independence of a thirty year old. Being sexualized at such as a young age puts me on the same plane as any adult. In some cases, I am above, more powerful than people I meet. I control them, manipulate them."

"Then, out of nowhere, my mother appears. We are downtown, in Allentown, shopping, and there in front of me is my mother, on the same street where I prostitute. I have not seen her in almost three years. She is alone, which is rare, no greasy man with her. I am with Jake, my greasy man. History does repeat itself. There is this very clumsy moment where Jake and my mom exchange glances. I am not sure what it is but there is a tension, perhaps a competitive little tug of war over me. My mother recognizes me immediately. Mom asks Jake if she and I can have some time alone. Jake agrees and my mother and I walk to the park in the middle of downtown, Victoria Park.

"It's uncomfortable. She explains how she was found by someone at the time of her father's, my grandfather's, passing. I hear about the funeral. There are some fake tears, from both of us. I get the sense there must have been some money involved, probably life insurance, because grandpa had nothing. I assume that mom took the money and went off on a bender with some loser. She must have known that I went into foster care. Where else would I have gone? She clearly made no effort to find me or collect me. I, at thirteen, can't confront her with my rage about being abandoned, repeatedly. I should be telling this person to go fly a kite, screw off, but I don't, I can't. There is an odd pull in me. The feeling is not familiar to me and I don't like it. It is an emotional vulnerability that goes against my gut feeling. My gut says, get as far away from this person as you possibly can, she will only hurt you, but my heart says, 'mommy'. There are obvious signs that tell me any contact with her will end badly."

"The biggest sign was that she does not ask about Jake, who he is, what I was doing with him. Here I am on the street with this guy, who at a minimum is pretty sketchy. He looks like a loser, a pimp and mommy doesn't ask if I am safe. She doesn't ask where I live, if I am eating well, where I have been, how I have survived. There is no motherly instinct there. She doesn't care. She is a poster child for narcissism. All she can talk about is herself and how my absence impacted her. I should run like hell. I should stab her with my knife, in the throat and watch her die, but I don't."

"I disclose the mechanics of where I have been but certainly no intimate details. It's a verbal bullet point review of my whereabouts over the past three years, the Coles Notes version. I get no details in return. That is a conversation killer. There are some big pauses, empty spaces in our conversation. I can tell she is reflecting and out of the blue she asks me if I want to come and live with her. I say yes. She writes down her address and phone number for me and I leave to go back to Jake's."

"Back at Jake's with a certain excitement I tell him that my mom wants me home and that I am going to go and live with her. Bang, the back of Jake's hand comes across my face knocking me to the floor. He jumps on top of me and begins punching me in the ribs and stomach. Pimps don't damage the face of their prostitutes. He is in a rage that I have never seen from him before. He sounds a lot like my grandfather with his insults, his name calling. Coughing up blood I am left on the floor. I can't move. Carolyn comes to my aid. She brings water and a towel. Jake leaves the apartment furious. Carolyn says, 'Are you out of your fucking mind? You can't leave. You belong to Jake. He has cared for you, groomed you, trained you. You are his income.' Carolyn very tenderly nurses me, holds me, speaks softly to me. I can tell that she loves me."

"I fall into a sleep, perhaps more like an unconsciousness. When I wakeup Jake is there, smiling. He has brought me pizza and a bracelet. He says that he is sorry but that I hurt him very deeply. He says that he loves me and that I am his family. It caught me off guard. It was strangely intense. I am confused emotionally and badly beaten physically. Jake takes me out, alone, to try and make it up to me. He buys me another tattoo on my back. It is a wonderful phoenix. He holds my hand while the work is done. It is on my right shoulder blade. Jake says it represents my rebirth. He makes me promise that I won't leave him. I promise. It is such a broad swing from the beating to this expression of attachment. It's all just so confusing."

"After a few days of healing, laying around the apartment, Jake says that he has a job for me. This of course means turning a trick. There is something about his presentation that worries me. He is too abrupt. His guilt from beating me is gone. The expression of caring is gone too. There is a detachment in his demeanour that rubs me wrong. My racing thoughts begin, uncontrollably."

"This worrying sends me to my knife, to cut, because I can't just go to Jake and resolve my feelings."

"I am working on my inner thigh, with great precision. I have a row of twelve cuts inside my right thigh and eight on my left. They are all the same, identical. They are the same length, the same width, the same depth. They are the same distance apart. They create the same scar. The cutting distracts me. It creates focus. It stops the racing thoughts, the worry. I take off my pants, sit on the floor in a Buddha position in my underwear and slowly carve a slit in my left leg. There is a rhythm to it, like a rocking chair or porch swing, gently rubbing the knife back and forth, watching the skin first become red, irritated then begin to split. There is very little blood drawn. The pain is splendour. Pain is my friend. It tells me that I am real, that I do exist, I am alive. It is a ritual. It's like being in outer space where everything else disappears, becomes insignificant. I dab the little bit of blood with a Kleenex, five times, it has to be five, looking each time at the little dot of blood on the tissue."

"Later, Jake comes to me and says it is time to work. Carolyn helps me get ready, makeup, hair, dress, nails. Carolyn tells me that I am special, that Jake treats me different than the other girls. She seems a little jealous. Carolyn has a worried look on her face. The whole thing has me completely baffled. I can't tell what is going on. I can't tell the good guys from the bad guys."

"As we walk with Jake he explains that it is an Oriental businessman from Hong Kong, in town for the weekend. I have been sold for three days and I will get one hundred dollars. I have hidden my mother's phone number and address from Jake in my pocket purse, in the liner. Jake takes me to a downtown hotel where outside we say good-bye to Carolyn. I can tell she is holding back tears. The hotel, the nicest hotel in Allentown is in front of us. I have never been in this hotel before. It is gorgeous, with a marble lobby, lofted ceilings, plush carpet, soft music.

I walk in with my weekend bag of clothes and supplies over my shoulder. We meet the Oriental man in the lobby between the bamboo trees and the wishing well. Jake has an odd exchange with the Oriental man. It is not the usual business transaction, payment, terms. It takes longer than usual, perhaps, I think a language issue. We go up to his room. Jake leaves without saying good-bye."

"The Chinaman speaks very little English. He tells me his name is Jimmy, smiling, squinting, bowing. Pornography is playing on the television with no sound. I suspect he has masturbated to get rid of that first easy one. The radio is playing. He begins to drink Scotch and so do I. I never get drunk while I am working. I need my wits about me. I am sitting in a chair. Jimmy is on the very soft bed. The room is just a room, your basic hotel room. There is a large bed, a nightstand, a desk with a chair, a large draped window, a double closet and a bathroom. The walls are a peach colour, the drapes brown. Jimmy is very unattractive, pimpled, balding, fat, short, Dumbo ears, little stubby fingers. It is clear that Jimmy wants his money's worth. He wants to get started. I am not there for company or conversation. He is getting loaded and he starts to strip. His gestures indicate that he wants me to strip too. Turning up the music on the radio, he is acting like a fool. I am holding back my laughter. It's the band, Chicago."

'Waiting for the break of day
Searching for something to say
Dancing lights against the sky
Giving up I close my eyes
Sitting cross-legged on the floor
25 or 6 to 4

Staring blindly into space
Getting up to splash my face
Wanting just to stay awake
Wondering how much I can take

Should have tried to do some more
25 or 6 to 4

Feeling like I ought to sleep
Spinning room is sinking deep
Searching for something to say
Waiting for the break of day
25 or 6 to 4
25 or 6 to 4'

    "Not exactly dance music, letting alone, stripper music. My internal alarms are going off like fireworks. There is something wrong with the whole scenario. Thoughts are racing through my head, terrible thoughts. I have this fleeting thought that Jake has sold me to this man, in total, sexual slavery. Then I think maybe Jake has paid this guy to get rid of me, kill me. I am searching the room for answers. Jimmy is drinking and dancing. It is really peculiar. I don't see any suitcases or clothes that would make this guy a businessman away from home on business. There are no suit bags, briefcases, car keys, rental car folders, nothing. I go to the bathroom. There are no tooth brushes, shaving kits, mouthwash, nothing. Now, I am scared. I am scared and I am looking for Skully. She is ready, as always and loaded for bear. Back in the room Jimmy is down to his tightey-whiteys, holding his Scotch and water in one hand, a cigarette in the other. Skully sees him as harmless, a drunken old Chinaman. She is not afraid. Skully takes off her shirt and joins the dancing. It is play time for Skully. She will go along with the Chinaman and tease his intentions out of him."

    "The Chinaman looks at Skully and stops dead in his tracks. He is staring at my stomach and chest. I completely forgot that I still have significant bruising from the beating Jake gave me. Jimmy goes off on a tirade, mostly in Chinese but I can hear in broken English, 'damaged goods, damaged goods.'"

    "The Chinaman charges at me all Kung Fu. The fat, round, short, drunk man falls on his face like Don Zimmerman. This is no killer assassin. In a flash, Skully pulls out the knife from her ankle sheath and plunges it in the Chinaman's back. I can hear the air coming out of his punctured lung like air out of a flat tire. Skully pulls out the knife and rams it into the back of his neck, right on the spine. He is done."

"Skully has no panic point. She is not scared, ready to run. She begins to look around, to figure out what the fuck is going on. It doesn't take her long. Opening the double bi-fold doors to the closet she finds a video camera on a tri pod. The red light is on and we have action. She breaks out in laughter. Jake, the Snake, 'what a gas!' she says out loud. Child porn, a new revenue stream for Jake, business is expanding. Skully pulls the video tape out of the camera and destroys it by pulling the tape out of its casing. She puts the whole mess in her bag to be dropped in a garbage bin later."

"Skully continues her room search. She pockets over three thousand dollars in cash found in the Chinaman's pants, a watch, a gold money clip, a pair of cuff links and the looting is over. Skully showers, cleans her knife and puts on the most child-like clothes she can find in her bag. She walks out the door. She came in all hookered up and left like a little girl looking for the indoor swimming pool."

"At a pay phone down the street I call my mother and arrange to meet her. Jake's is not an option. I don't even try to figure out what that whole scene was about with the Chinaman, the camera, the money. I never did sort that out. I sleep at my mother's house that night."

Dr. Colby closes with, "Am I correct that you, during all this time, since leaving the foster home, living with Jake, you are not in school?"

I react, "Correct, no school, no tutoring, no formal education. I am getting a different kind of education, the education of the street, Street U. No one has ever read me a story, sang to me in the bathtub, skipped with me, taught me to draw on a driveway with chalk. I have seen these things in windows of houses, in neighbourhoods, as I travel to a secluded area to give some sexually frustrated husband a blow job."

Chapter Thirteen

The Cavalry

Being unwanted, unloved, uncared for, forgotten by everybody, I think that is a much greater hunger, a much greater poverty than the person who has nothing to eat.
– Mother Teresa

The Salvation Army Church is not at all like the shelter. It is faith- based care as opposed to man hating-based care. I am an equal opportunity hater. I hate everyone. I trust no one. The Army is far less intrusive than the shelter. They don't want to case manage me. They would like to save me, but in a salvation, spiritual kind of way. Their care is for the homeless with no gender bias. They accept men and women. Their facility has separate areas for gender privacy but the sleeping arrangements are more akin to an army barracks than a home atmosphere. The Army is military in many ways. There are rows of beds and group showers. Their only expectation is that you are in the building by six o'clock to secure your bed. They hold prayer, host AA meetings, have bible study and full church services on Sundays. There aren't a lot of questions asked. It is a church where you are given sanctuary. If you go to them, they will help, but they are not ramming it down your throat.

I am a born again Atheist. Every time I get near God, I get disappointed in some way, not that I have been anywhere near God. There is no God. God would not allow a ten-year-old child to have a cane shoved up her ass by her drunken grandfather. No one would be shitting on my face if there were a God. I have faith in nothing and no one.

I left the shelter with only the clothes on my back. I went to the shelter to catch my breath after three years on the street. I was worn out, exhausted. I had hoped to get my bearings, clean up, hide and move on. The recent events have set me back. In fact, I am farther behind than when I arrived at the women's shelter. Dr. Colby has also factored into my decision to remain in Allentown. Our sessions are helping me, emotionally.

My statistics include two kills while in the shelter. I cut the head off that case manager bitch Janice and bashed in the skull of that arrogant executive director. It seems there is no escape for me. I have lost count but I believe Skully and I are up to thirty kills. In some circles I would be considered a serial killer. However, my profile is different, I think, because I am not a predator. Patrolling, trolling, targeting, planning are not my thing. There are no trophies, no fingers in the fridge, no heads in the freezer, no eating body parts, no hiding and revisiting bodies, no post mortem sexual fetishes. I don't write to the newspaper or taunt the police. I am not on a mission to cleanse the world of prostitutes, or eliminate horny teenage boys from the planet. I have no agenda, just don't fuck with me and we will be fine.

My mess of a life just seems to put me in circumstances where killing seems a logical decision, a good outcome, a necessity. I live a very risky life. I am in risky places, with risky people, doing risky things and this has been the case for thirty years. From that perspective it is only one kill a year. There have been years where I killed no one. There was no need. They seem to happen in bunches. At this time, I would say that I am on a roll. I don't get caught because by and large I don't exist and the world I live in does not exist. There is no family to suspect me, or report me. I have never had a job or a Social Insurance Number. I have never had a driver's licence, a credit card or even a permanent address. I have never collected welfare, filed an income tax return or had an OHIP card.

I need to stay away from hospitals, because they have a record of me. I need to stay out of jail or police custody because I have a criminal record and I need to stay clear of Children's Aid Society, because they have a record of me. I live, as they say, off the grid. I am a ghost. I can vanish in a second. I live by my wits, street smarts, instinct. I have no real regard for others. I have no attachments. I steal, lie, cheat, manipulate, kill, to survive. This pessimistic, negative outlook on life, on human nature, puts me close to suicide. I have a long history of self harm, cutting, tattooing. At this point in time I am burnt out. This is a sort of mid-life crisis. I see no purpose, no reason to live. There is no future for me. When I look back I see a whole lot of misery. When I look at where I am now I see emptiness. When I look ahead I see no goals, no dreams, nothing. In a sense I am at peace with the idea of killing myself. This is not going to be done in a fit of rage or in deep despair. It is an ending that I embrace. It is a natural outcome to the life that I have led. I just have one loose end to tie up.

Setting up shop at the Army allows me to maintain my anonymity, to fly under the radar. I know these systems, resources, how they function, what they can do for me, all across Canada and the United States.

Chapter Fourteen

Grass in the Kitchen

I don't know the key to success, but the key to failure is trying to please everybody.
– Bill Cosby

I look forward to seeing Dr. Colby. It is like an emotional downloading that frees up space in my head. Sometimes I think it is driven by other psychological needs. My suicidal thinking seems to play a role in this need. It's like a need to reconcile some things before I leave the planet, dare I say confess my sins. I really can't go to that extreme because I have left out details while sharing my history with Dr. Colby. He is not getting the full story. I am always holding back, protecting myself. Back in the well-adorned doctor's office we have been through our greeting ritual and I am off with the next chapter in the saga.

"I have bailed on Jake and the hippy group leaving a dead Chinaman behind. I am at my mother's. This is my mother who has not really raised me. I lived with my grandfather while my mother went through a series of losers, who beat her, stole from her, cheated on her and ultimately left her. She chose them over me. Mom would visit me and grandpa from time to time. I watched her snort cocaine, inject heroin, down percs and oxys like candy, and pot, lots and lots of marijuana."

"I am not sure what to expect from my mom as we set up house. She is living in a cute two-bedroom little cottage in Allentown, off the main core area of town. It is an old home with plaster walls, a fireplace, a dirt basement and a boiler for heat. It is tastefully decorated and the furniture is clean. The space speaks to a contentment that I have not seen out of my mother. This is not the flop house, mess I have visited her in before. My mom tells me that she took the insurance money from grandpa's passing and bought the house. She says that she used it to turn her life around. I am thinking perhaps this is what she needed to get her act together, but I am thirteen or fourteen, what do I know, really? But, it does seem that mom's lot in life has improved."

"My mom doesn't ask how I have been, what my life has been like. It seems like she doesn't want to know. She doesn't want to know because it will make her feel guilty. Hearing the details of my life, would confirm for her that she has been a horrible mother. Further, there are few details coming from her to me, concerning what she has been up to. I can only imagine what that means, what any of it might mean. We are living in the here and now. It is a sort of wiping the slate clean start, a Mulligan, a redo, but it's not real. We have no real attachment to one another and that becomes obvious. Intellectually mom understood that she needed to parent me, emotionally, her heart was not in it. As time went on I realized that what mom had was living the same miserable, narcissistic life just in a better wrapper. You can take the princess out of the slum but you can't take the slum out of the princess. There were chinks in the armour. After a few days, I realized mommy dear was not going to work, there was no legitimate job. She bought and decorated a home but how was she maintaining it, paying the bills? Soon I realized how, she was selling pot out of her cutely decorated country kitchen. Now, I am home. The side door is forever opening and closing, customers, arriving, departing. It's not the street sleaze clientele though. These customers are a more upscale group, well dressed, good smelling, articulate people. For all the protests, the screw authority bad attitude, the don't trust anyone over the age of thirty, the hippies did become the yuppies. They did find jobs, careers, homes, BMWs but what they did not lose was their love of pot, marijuana. Mom had found a little niche market in the upper middle class potheads of Allentown. It was perfect, discreet, no risk, no credit, all cash. It wasn't a heat score. A heat score is a situation that is going to bring heat, the police, to your door, for something. Some of her customers are cops. Mom isn't hiding this little business from me but we are also not discussing it. It is a sort of open secret."

"Mom, Doris, has no idea how to parent. She is not enrolling me in school, getting me a family doctor, dentist, library card. I know it is only a matter of time and then it happens, like this, 'Margaret can you do something for me? Can you take something to the bus station and bring back a package for me?' This little request doesn't fool or surprise me. I know how the world works, quid pro quo, you scratch my back and I scratch yours, nobody rides for free. Doris is providing me with a place to stay. In my spare time I work on my art, drawing. I need to earn my keep, just like at Jakes. I get it. This is an easy request. I have smuggled drugs across an international border. This is a simple drop off and pick up. It's a cool little system actually because it is done with lockers at the bus terminal. You are not meeting a person. You take a locker key to the bus terminal, open the locker, remove a gym bag of drugs, take the key you find in the locker and put the money in the locker, then hide that key in an agreed upon spot. There is a lot of trust involved, so you know this is a higher level group of people. These are not nervous, paranoid people with guns."

"Mom seems to have broken her vulnerability to scumbag men, shattered it really. There are no hangers on, no bullies shouting obscenities, no lunatics with hand guns, no stalking, phoning. Ellen is the only person that comes around. She is a little younger than my mom. They hang out, smoke a little product and chill. Ellen and Doris go out from time to time, to movies, or concerts or to see bands at bars. Ellen does work, a real job. She has a job as a legal secretary in a law firm in Allentown. Ellen is legit, straight up, educated, has an apartment, goldfish and a cat. She is hot, smartly dressed with an athletic body. She has the most amazing shoes. It is clear she has not been beaten up by the world. Her skin is amazing, soft, clear, healthy. Her voice is like music. Ellen treats me really well. An amateur photographer, she takes pictures, my picture. She talks to me, plays cards with me, even Monopoly. We learn to play chess together."

"For all my street smarts it takes me about six months to figure out that Doris and Ellen are lesbian lovers. Well, I don't figure it out really, I interrupt them in full glory, tearing one off at lunch time. I returned early from a drop off and leave outing. There they were. They were so invested, they didn't see me, but I saw them. Doris had gone gay."

"I didn't confront them. I left well enough alone. It was kind of sweet. We were in the mid-seventies so there were few, if any, openly gay couples. It was all still in the closet, at least in Allentown. We were not in San Francisco. We were in Allentown, Ontario. Doris had created a real little empire with the help of Ellen. Doris was Ellen's bad girl. Ellen was Doris's connection to the upper crust of Allentown. The lawyer in Ellen's office connected other lawyers, accountants, doctors, bankers to Doris. It was brilliant. Doris had the perfect market for her illegal product. She was selling to professionals. She was making enough money to keep the house going and have some fun. There were no cottages in Muskoka or boats in Toronto Harbour but it was good, above the trailer park life she grew up in."

"So, Dr. Colby, how does this go bad? You know that it must. What is your guess?"

Dr. Colby, in a very serious tone says, "I don't want to guess Margaret. Each week you up the ante on a life that is one crisis after another. I don't know how you have kept one foot in front of the other all these years. Your life would have killed me, years ago. I could not have endured, survived, what you have been through, honestly. I am so impressed with your resiliency, your strength. You have had your challenges, but here you are. For a person with no formal education, you are bright, expressive. It is a honour to know you. Our time is up and I will keep the suspense alive to see how Doris and Ellen turn this for the worst. I also wanted to say that I noticed no Skully yet, while at your mother's. It is clear to me that Skully is that warrior part of your personality that emerges when you are threatened. For future reference, you should think that Skully is part of you. She is not a separate you. Margaret and Skully co-exist. The treatment for this involves the integration of both personalities into one, not the elimination of one or the other. I will see you next week, good-bye."

Chapter Fifteen

Wanna Bet

Gambling: The sure way of getting nothing from something.
– Kane Mizner

"Dr. Colby? Are you ready? I think you will like this chapter of my life. My life had brushed me up against many extremes; violence, guns, addictions, self harm, betrayals, abandonment had all been part of my young life. Addictions come in many forms and I have seen them all, shopping, sex, fitness, alcohol, money, work, drugs, gambling, video games. Doris, my mother, appeared to be doing so much better, compared to when I was living in the trailer with my grandfather. However, as they say, appearances can be deceiving. Sometimes it's about what you don't see as opposed to what you do see. I am living with my mother and I don't see any heroin, cocaine, LSD, valium or anything hard at the house, just pot and tobacco. I never saw any needles, spoons, crack pipes or other hard drug paraphernalia. There are no sketchy, dangerous, risky people around. However, over time it became apparent to me that my mom had developed another problem. Mom had replaced her hard drug use with another addiction, gambling."

"My mom should not have money. She has no idea how to handle it, budget, save. She would not be satisfied with a little life insurance money. She would want more, that is what addicts do. They have no common sense, no filter in their brain that says, that's enough, stop right there. Doris had an influx of cash that allowed her to dig herself out of a huge hole. She had the resources to make substantial changes in her life, her lifestyle. Probably the greatest advancement, change, was that she was no longer dependent on anyone. She did not need a slimeball boyfriend to support her. The life insurance money bought her a house and a lifestyle that she could never have imagined."

"Doris, on drugs, with an abusive boyfriend, was heading full speed towards being dead in a ditch. She was either going to be beaten to death by some lunatic boyfriend, or accidentally overdose on drugs, then God smiled on her. He gave her a second chance. He lifted her up out of that mess of a life she had been living and put her in a better place. But, addicts, Doris, can't stand prosperity.

They don't know when they have it good. They are empty and need to be filled up, but at the same time they are cracked, leaking, so they need to be filled up again, and again. This is not a good place to be and Doris was in the middle of it."

"I have walked away from drugs and alcohol many times in my life. I don't seem to have that purely addictive part to my personality. I just have Skully. She would kick my ass if I got hooked on something or someone. Skully is my filter. That's not to say that I have not used substances for therapeutic purposes."

"I start to hear Doris and Ellen fighting, fucking lesbian bitches. They are a married, bickering, couple. There are two issues that they are fighting about, me and gambling. Ellen wants me in school. She is my step-mother now. Imagine that, for most of my life I have no mother, now, I have two mommies. Wouldn't that have been fun to explain at school on family day:

'This is my mommy and this is my other mommy. There was a sperm donor somewhere, but this is my family. This mommy sells dope and this mommy works for a lawyer.'

Ellen wants me in public school. Ellen wants to replicate her childhood for me. Ellen grew up riding horses, taking dance lessons and having tea parties. While Ellen was riding horses, Doris was riding cowboys, if you catch my drift. I am Ellen's chance to be a mother, to parent, to be a nurturer and she has a different model of mother than Doris. It is at this time that I begin to menstruate. It's Ellen who teaches me how to look after myself, not my mother."

"The second issue for debate is gambling. Ellen does not agree with Doris's gambling. She feels it is out of control. Doris is not an occasional, recreational gambler. She is not taking her recreational dollar and betting at the racetrack, then coming home. She is taking huge risks. Doris has a bookie. She is betting on sports, baseball, football, hockey, basketball, out of control."

"I don't know what the deal is between Doris and Ellen, but they are entrenched enough that neither walks away from the relationship, despite the fighting. They are committed to one another. There is no deal breaker here. They fight, argue, but the gambling will not end their relationship and neither will I. I know if it were me, I would be out. 'If you don't like it, screw off!'"

"However, like most addicts, Doris is also minimizing her gambling losses to Ellen. The house that had been paid for now has a mortgage. Doris is losing, losing everything. Then the wheels really start to come off."

"First, two very large men come to the house to visit Doris. I am sent to my room. I hear shouting, threats. Then a few days later, Doris comes home with a cast on her arm. She tries to float a bullshit story about falling. No, she has been muscled. The walls are coming down, closing in on Doris. Ellen doesn't buy the story about the broken arm. There was no fall. I don't buy it either, but no one confronts Doris. We joke, sign the cast. It's all funny. Doris had a good thing, a house, a home, a lifestyle and she fucked it all up. She had the little cottage, a nice little illegal income, a good partner, Ellen, that cared for her, her daughter back and it all blows up in her face, over money."

"Then on one of my runs to the bus station I am grabbed, kidnapped. It is my usual duty, my job, my contribution. I am doing my weekly walk up to the bus station. It's not a large bus station. There are maybe five buses there at any given time, old, dirty, diesel, Greyhound buses. The bus station is more of a shelter, a single large room. There is a bank of lockers at one end, a ticket window, benches to sit on and a concession stand in the middle. There are posters advertising Coca Cola, AC Spark Plugs, Double Bubble Gum and Maxwell House Coffee."

"On this day, entering the bus shelter, as I approach the locker I see someone leaning against the lockers. He is a big man with a long leather coat. He is wearing a bowler style hat, a derby and gloves. He doesn't look out of place in the bus station. It seems like no big deal, clearly he is not a cop. As I put my key in the locker he grabs my arm, hard. He is a big strong dude and he is guiding, dragging me outside. Skully won't scream. She is too tough for that. We are outside as a panel van pulls up and boom, the door slides open, I am in the back of the van on the floor. The big strong guy follows me into the vehicle. I am a little shaken but not stirred. I am trying to get my bearings. This can't be about the drugs because the big goof didn't empty the locker or take my duffle bag of money. I still have it. He didn't know what I was doing at the bus station."

"Looking around I can see that there is a driver, a guy in the back and the goon that grabbed me and shoved me in. The guy in the back says, 'Relax, we don't want to hurt you, but your mother owes our boss a lot of money. We just want to scare her and get her to pay us what she owes.'

"Dr. Colby, at this point I am fourteen or fifteen years old. I am still a little waif of a girl, less than five feet tall, under ninety pounds all wet, but in my head, I am forty and not to be fucked with. You described Skully as a warrior. You were right."

"The fun starts as the big guy who grabbed me says, 'Why aren't you crying little girl?'

'Because you didn't hurt me you big fuck.'

'What did you say to me?'

'I said, that you are big fuck and I am not afraid of you.'

'Did you hear that Jeff? I should pound this little bitch.'"

"The driver is clearly the leader, he is pissed, 'Shut up, no names you asshole. She is just a little girl. Leave her alone. We need her. She is going to talk to her mom, we will get the money, then we will dump her.'"

"The goon climbs into the front of the van and takes a seat. I can tell we are on the highway now. We are moving pretty fast. I surmise that we are leaving Allentown. My mind is racing. I really didn't like the sound of 'we will dump her' and neither did Skully. These are not the days of cell phones, so we need to stop if I am going to talk to my mom. They need a land line."

"Looking around the old panel van, it's pretty empty. There are two seats at the front of the cab for the driver and one passenger, then a metal floor. There is a side, sliding door and rear doors. There are no windows in the back, on the walls or back doors. The radio is playing, Elvis,

'You know I can be found,
sitting home all alone,
If you can't come around,
at least please telephone.
Don't be cruel to a heart that's true.

Baby, if I made you mad
for something I might have said,
Please, let's forget the past,
the future looks bright ahead.
Don't be cruel to a heart that's true.
I don't want no other love,
Baby it's just you I'm thinking of.'"

"No one is holding me. I am not tied or restrained, as kidnappers go, they aren't very good at this. What is a good kidnapping without duct tape? I try to move to see if they will stop me. They don't. I slide to the side of the van with no door and push my back up against the side of the van. One bad guy is right behind the driver on his knees looking forward, occasionally glancing back to see what I am up to. He is generally ignoring me. I guess he figures I won't jump out because we are moving too fast and I am a little tart of a thing, who can I hurt? The other guy has climbed into the passenger seat. The threat is real and Skully is plotting a response."

"We have been driving, fast, on a highway, for maybe half an hour. I assume we are going to Toronto. I am trying to process all this. These guys, I am thinking, have made a critical strategic error. They assume that my mom will care that they have grabbed me and pay. I don't think so. Ellen might, but she isn't likely to hear about any of this until it is too late."

"Skully has had enough. It is time to take control of the situation. Sitting against the side wall of the van she pulls her legs up to her bum. The incompetent kidnappers did not search me. With one eye on the guy kneeling behind the driver, Skully pulls out her knife. She feels the beauty, the strength of the sharp weapon in her hand and she lunges at him. She stabs him in the neck. Pulling the knife out she flips the knife around and with a back hand slice catches the passenger in the throat with her blade. The van starts to weave. Skully goes back to the man on the floor and jabs her knife deep into his chest. The van is out of control, swerving and then there is a crash. We hit another vehicle, sideswiping them. Skully is tossed like a salad bouncing around the back of the van. There are tires screeching, horns blowing and then the brakes. Skully is thrown forward and bounces off the back of the seats. Her knife is sticking out of the chest of the man on the floor. The passenger is alive but without a seatbelt he has bashed his head off the windshield as a result of the crash. Skully pulls the knife out of the man's chest and thrusts it cruelly into the back of the passenger. The driver is focussed on trying to control the van. He is swearing and rolling around in his seat, his hands fixed to the steering wheel. Stopping isn't really an option. He keeps driving trying to regain control of the van. Skully moves and stands on the back of the man on the floor. She reaches around the driver with her knife and slits his throat from ear to ear. Skully can see now, out the front windshield and the van is headed for the ditch on the side of the road. The van has slowed because of the collision with the other vehicle, the brakes and the driver had let his foot off the gas. In the ditch it simply slows in the long wet grass and stops."

"There is no panic in Skully. She searches each of the three men. She collects about eighteen hundred dollars in cash, a couple of gold rings and a couple of watches. She stills has the duffle bag of drug money, twenty five thousand dollars in cash. Skully slides open the side door of the van, pokes her head out and, not seeing anything, jumps out into the wet grass. Excited she walks up the slight grade to the service road that runs parallel to the highway."

"Free, she is walking, in the direction of Toronto. Glancing around Skully sees nothing that would represent a threat or worry. We walked for maybe a mile with the duffle bag. I could hear sirens approaching. I wasn't sure what to do. There was no fear, simply a decision to make. Should I continue to Toronto or get back on the other side of the highway and go back to Allentown. In the end I saw no good reason to return to Allentown. My brief stay with mom had proven to be a disaster. She is still not the mother of the year. I certainly did not want to hook up with Jake again. Foster care did not seem like a good option. So I closed the chapter on Allentown and headed towards Toronto. We are in the seventies so hitchhiking is still acceptable, common. I walked to the next highway on-ramp and held out my thumb. Within five minutes I was in a car on my way to Toronto."

"I feel excited, invigorated, I have almost thirty grand in cash. I am not destitute. I have resources, skills and a plan. I also have a partner, Skully."

Dr. Colby interrupts, "Our time is up Margaret. Your story continues to impress me. Your survival instinct is certainly strong. Skully is a real asset. She is not dominating you. It's like you call on her in circumstances that you need her. Again, the goal is to accept her as part of you, to integrate your personalities into one. Margaret, you are confessing some very serious crimes here. I am bound by confidentiality. I can't disclose anything without your permission. You are particularly safe because there is no immediate danger to you or anyone else in what you have said. If I thought you were going to harm yourself, now, I would have a professional obligation to do something. I will see you next week."

Chapter Sixteen

Despair is the Absence of Hope

If they tell you that she died of sleeping pills you must know that she died of a wasting grief, of a slow bleeding at the soul.
– Clifford Odets

The Salvation Army Church Hostel is a real asset to me. I fit myself into their rules and expectations perfectly to raise no eyebrows. They understand three hots and a cot, perfectly. They don't pressure me and I actually enjoy the bible study, the church services. I still keep to myself. There is no interaction with other residents. They turn over much quicker than at the women's shelter. The faces don't remain the same.

I have no capacity for compassion. Nothing pulls on my heart strings. I lack the ability to put myself in someone else's shoes and see the world from their perspective. Many of the other residents look pathetic, unhealthy, dirty, the classic dishevelled homeless look. I may look exactly as they do. Clearly some of these people have mental health issues. They talk to themselves, hear voices, even hallucinate. Back in the day we had bums and hobos. Now we have the homeless. They have status.

There is a physician that visits the hostel. I believe his name is Dr. Pindall. He is a Doogie Howser fellow looking fresh out of medical school, finding his way with his white lab coat, stethoscope around his neck and pocket of pens, with a tiny little flashlight. He is from a community health clinic, a cute energetic little fellow with light brown hair, blue eyes and a perfect teeth kind of a smile. They don't ask for a health card. It's free, accessible health care. Every Tuesday the doctor comes and spends the day. It's different from anything I have ever experienced before. He is there, available, relaxed, just looking to be helpful. He is not like other doctors, shoving patients through every fifteen minutes to maximize income, making you feel like you have annoyed them by needing their care.

I am afraid to have a physical, afraid of what they may find. With the life that I have led there is no way I can be healthy. I have issues that I have just ignored, worked around, learned to endure. I have blood in my urine. It burns when I pee. My vision is poor. I lose my breath easily. There is a large lump on my right side just below my last rib. I am passively suicidal which means I don't care if I live or die so I don't responsibly care for myself. Part of my courage comes from my attitude. I don't care if I live or die. Beyond that there are moments when I am actively suicidal. I plan my own ending. I have the thoughts, the plan and the means. I honestly don't know why I don't kill myself. I see no reason to go on living. I wake up, fumble through a day, wait to die. It is the essence of depression. I should bring this up with Dr. Colby, but I am afraid. I am afraid of being put in hospital, against my will. There are some things, said out loud, that send the world into a tizzy. So these thoughts are better off just bouncing around in my head, unspoken, locked up in the vault. It is strange, even to me, how I have left the shelter, arrived at the hostel and not really even skipped a beat. These thoughts, feelings are also locked up in my head. Suppression is an art form. For most people the recent events in my life would be a crisis, not for me. The events themselves are a crisis, but I am not in crisis. Crisis is the absence of coping skills and I am coping just fine, thankyou. I find a way. This is my talent. I find a way to survive, to get through, to move on and I don't really look back. It's like I can erase my personal history. I don't drag things forward with me. I have no baggage. I could also be accused of not looking ahead either. I function in this survival mode, almost all the time. Never have I been stable, settled, planning where I might go or what I might do. My life has been just one crisis situation after another. I have done what I have had to, to survive, then I have moved on. This is why my sessions with Dr. Colby are so helpful. I have never told the story before, from beginning to end, the story of my life, not even to myself. Now, though, it is like I am running out of gas, the will is gone, the fight has left me. I feel like I should surrender. This is what has me in the hostel. I am out of gas and I need to recharge my batteries, lick some wounds, get my shit together.

Chapter Seventeen

Ink

He who has a why to live can bear almost any how.
– Friedrich Nietzsche

"Dr. Colby? I must be getting better. I am actually thinking about our sessions in between sessions," I offer looking around the plush office.

"What have you been thinking Margaret?" Dr. Colby responds.

"Well, I was thinking that my life has been one crisis after another. I have been in survival mode virtually my whole, entire life," I explain.

"True, Margaret and survive you have. I have said this to you before. You have a resiliency that is so impressive, second to none that I have ever seen. Your life would have killed me, long ago. I am weak, compared to you. However, life too has a way of catching up to you. You can only function the way that you have for so long before the whole thing sneaks up behind you and bites you on the ass." The doctor suggests a clinical opinion.

"I feel that, I feel tired, I feel worn out. Something has compelled me to return to Allentown, where it all began. Something compels me to come here and tell you my story. Something compels me to stay at the hostel and rest. Shall I carry on my story?" I ask.

"If that is how you want to spend our time, yes, by all means, carry on," the doctor responds.

"OK. I was kidnapped by the Three Stooges, Curly, Larry and Moe. Escaping, I found myself in a car on my way to Toronto. I had a bag of cash, some thirty g's and of course no real plan. Briefly, and I mean briefly, I thought about my mom and Ellen. Taking mother's thirty thousand dollars would make her life more difficult but in an alcoholic logic model, I rationalized that she owed me this money. She had not been a good mother to me. She put me at risk leaving me with a drunken abusive grandfather. She dumped me in foster care, twice. Between the gambling debt and now the missing thirty grand in drug money, she was in deep shit. She deserved it. This was a debt owed to me, retribution. I did not lose any sleep over taking the money. The way the kidnapping ended it is possible mom thought that I had just taken off with the money.

She may never have learned that I was kidnapped."

"As I stepped out of my ride on to Yonge Street in downtown Toronto I was in awe, the city lights, Sam the Record Man, the Eaton's Centre, the Zanzibar Circus, the buskers, the noise, the traffic, the hoards of people. It was overwhelming and I was taking it all in. I sat in front of the Eaton's Centre just people watching for over an hour, then I started to walk. Walking, north, towards Bloor Street I saw the occasional sign, in a sunken doorway, 'apartment for rent'. They were for little studio apartments above the street, above stores, shops, bars. Then I saw a sign that said, 'furnished apartment'. Climbing the narrow, steep stairs, I had a good feeling. It was a two room, one bathroom dive of a place, but it was heavenly. It was maybe three hundred dollars a month and I paid for six months in cash, in advance, my first place of my own, thankyou Curly, Larry and Moe. The bedroom was barely big enough for the bed, jammed in the corner. The window opened up right on to Yonge Street. I was above an Army Surplus Store, my new fashion influence. There was a small living room with an armchair, a loveseat and a coffee table. There was a small fridge and a hotplate in the living room. The floor was hardwood, the walls plaster, painted a shallow green. The bathroom had an old claw foot tub but no shower, a toilet and a sink. It was home. I felt good. I felt something that I had not felt before that moment, some amount of control. I had my own space, not someone's trailer, not a foster home, not a slimeball's apartment, my own home."

"My first order of business was to hide my cash. The bathroom had a little crawl space in it through the ceiling, a trap door of sorts. I put the cash in a paper bag and hid it in the rafters. Then I began to explore my new environment, neighbourhood. I felt such power walking through downtown Toronto tapping my pocket to check on my apartment key. I found a little market and bought some milk, some fruit and bread. In a second hand store I bought some dishes, knives, forks, a spoon, a pot, a frying pan, a glass and a cup. I am nesting. I own stuff. For that first week or so I didn't really speak to anyone but as time went by some of the faces began to develop a familiarity. I began to talk, ask people their names, the guy at the market, the man selling newspapers, the clerk at the second hand store. Exploring further, I began to identify things that I recognized, prostitution, drug selling, pick pockets, petty crime. It's amazing what you can see if you pay attention and you know what to look for. My time clock shifted, I was up all night, asleep all day. No one bothered me, I didn't seem out of place, despite my age. I looked much older. Life had worn on me. It was such a mass of humanity on the street, no one seemed to notice one little girl. I became part of the landscape."

"I used to watch the bus station. There were recruiters there looking for young girls getting off the bus, runaways, little girls that were sick of their stepfathers feeling them up at night. The recruiters would offer them a place to stay, to feed them, to protect them, get them high, hooked on drugs, then bully them into prostitution. I knew that game. I could see the full business on Church Street. I knew the drug game too, that was everywhere."

"I was not a waitress, a dishwasher, a busboy or a retail clerk. I knew that. I knew what I didn't want to do. I didn't know what to do. I had some ideas but I was not under any pressure to do anything. I had lots of cash. I could do absolutely nothing for a couple of years if I wanted to and still get by."

"It was at this time, as I ventured around this new world, that I found my tattoo parlour just off of Yonge Street. I arrived in Toronto with two tats. I had a spider on my hand, near my thumb and a phoenix on my right shoulder blade. I loved that tattoo parlour, the look of it, the smell of it, the taste of it. I loved being surrounded by creativity, drawings, sketches, paintings. It was at this time, as I am settling into Toronto, that I got my 'vine' tattoo that wraps around my body. I love that tat. It starts at my right ear and wraps around me seven times before it stops at my left ankle. It represents growth, being whole, wraparound. I love the green, the red, the yellow of it. I love looking at it when I am naked. I twirl around in front of a mirror to see all of it. It is amazing, whole body art. There were three artists in the tattoo parlour. It was called Tattoo You. I started to hang out there. The guys loved me, Mitch, Rider and Gus. They all had their own style and their own ink. They did each other, when it was slow or they were bored or high. They came up with designs, ideas. Mitch was a little skinny former heroin addict. He had a big eyeball tattooed on each of his knees. It was really weird. When you sat with him, in his shorts, you didn't know which set of eyes to look at, the ones in his head or the ones on his knees. If you looked down at his knees he would say you were looking at his balls and laugh a big beautiful laugh. Rider had his entire bald head and face tattooed down to his neck. It looked like he was wearing a mask. He also had horns, implants, at the top of his forehead. He really freaked people out. The stares were so intense but he was a beautiful person inside, kind, generous. Gus was a biker and had tribal tattoos before anyone even knew what they were. These guys became like brothers to me. They let me hang out in their shop and I helped out, sterilizing needles, cleaning up, doing the cash register, organizing the T-Shirts that they sold. In return I got free tattoos. It was cool, really cool. I was getting sleeved, from my shoulders to my hands, ink. They didn't ask questions about me and I didn't ask questions about them. They did a pretty good business, primarily by referral, from happy customers. There were no real hours of business, walk in or bang on the door. We got to meet some really cool people, even some famous people. We gave tattoos to Randy Bachman, Ramon McGuire of Trooper, Ritchie Henman of April Wine, Bill Henderson of Chilliwack and other Canadian musicians. This led to connections for concert tickets, backstage passes and huge parties. I saw the Rolling Stones and the Who at Maple Leaf Gardens in 1975."

"Music was always playing in the tattoo shop. The Who,
'I've looked under chairs
I've looked under tables
I've tried to find the key
To fifty million fables
They call me The Seeker
I've been searching low and high
I won't get to get what I'm after
Till the day I die
I asked Bobby Dylan
I asked The Beatles
I asked Timothy Leary
But he couldn't help me either'"

"I was never more at peace than I was in those first few months that I lived in Toronto. It was like I grew up, came of age. It was some kind of right of passage to another phase in my life. I never saw Skully. There was no need for her. I was sleeping for eight hours at a time. I stopped pulling out my hair. I felt whole. It was an amazing lifestyle, rock bands, music, discos, tattoos, Yonge Street in the seventies."

"My network of friends was expanding. I began to say hello to the doormen at the hotels in the downtown core. The cabbies that worked the area were folded into my rolodex of acquaintances. The security guards at Maple Leaf Gardens started letting me in to Leaf Games. I became a huge fan. One of my tats is a Maple Leaf. I got some great autographs on hockey cards, Darryl Sittler, Lanny McDonald, Tiger Williams, Borje Salming. I even had a pyramid in my apartment, pyramid power. There were some great games then against the Flyers, the Canadians, the Bruins. I still love hockey."

"The lads, Mitch, Rider and Gus had been encouraging me to draw, sketch. I was pretty shy at first, reluctant to express myself in this temple of creativity. The guys really encouraged me. They were teaching me, fostering my young talent and I was developing. I learned the arts of onion paper, charcoal sketching, water colours. After a while I had my own little collection of sketches, a portfolio, paintings and of course tattoo designs. I gave myself a couple of tats, on my thighs. They turned out pretty good. I did a small dragon on one leg and a butterfly on the other. I know, Doctor, you will like the Skully—Dragon and Margaret—Butterfly symbolism. Mitch liked my dragon and asked me to do the dragon on his ankle, I did. Now I was working legit in the tattoo parlour getting the occasional customer. My talent was emerging, developing, growing. My status was apprentice."

"Girls began coming into the shop and asking for me. I can do a rose on a breast in ten minutes. I was developing a clientele and a referral base. For the first time in my life I felt that I was capable of something, I was good at something. I had a career goal. My goal was to be the best female tattoo artist in Toronto. My mentors encouraged me, trained me, challenged me and I became a better artist. The walls in my little apartment were covered with drawings. Men and women began coming into the shop asking for my services. This was about a two year apprenticeship. By the time I turned sixteen I was a fixture on the Toronto Street scene. I was a walking billboard for the Tattoo You shop and had a steady stream of customers. Mitch, Rider and Gus helped me and I paid them a rental amount for working in the shop, like renting a chair in a beauty salon. I bought my own supplies and carried my own weight. The money that I brought to Toronto went down a bit but I began to float my own boat. I was making more than I was spending and building my nest egg back up. I wasn't getting rich but I was paying my own freight and setting a little aside. I couldn't open a bank account. I had no identification, no birth certificate, not even a student card."

"One day, Mitch came to me and said that there was someone that he wanted me to meet. It was Bert Grimm. Bert had taught and mentored Mitch. Bert was a legend in the tattoo world. He was originally from Oregon but had worked all over the United States as a tattoo artist before settling into Nu Pike, Long Beach, California. When I met him, he was an older gentlemen, in the sunset of his career, looking to define his legacy. Bert had worked on thousands of navy sailors before they shipped out to sea. Nu Pike was an amusement park dating back to the late 1800s. Tattooing was part of the park experience and the shop there was home to hundreds of tattoo artists dating back to the original days of the park, known as The Nu. At the time I didn't have the history or context to appreciate who I was meeting. I have been told that I had met the Elvis of the tattoo world, pretty impressive. Bert looked at my portfolio of work. He was impressed. I could tell. He kept looking at me, looking at my work, shaking his head and saying, 'fuck' in the most complimentary meaning of the word. Bert was in and out of the shop for over two weeks. He was doing tats, teaching us, mentoring me and then he made me a proposal. Bert, with Mitch's blessing, asked me to come to California with him, to work and train. He said that he had never had a female apprentice but that my talent exceeded my age. Bert said he wanted to leave, as part of his legacy one Canadian female artist. Bert said he was spreading his work like a venereal disease. Today the magnitude of that is much larger than it was then. There was no pressure to decide that minute. Bert left it with me, and Mitch. It was to be a three month internship with Bert and his shop."

"Mitch, Rider and Gus were so funny. They figuratively had my bags packed and my plane ticket bought. They didn't see any need for ambivalence. They were jumping up and down. The meaning of this to them was perfectly clear. To them I had been touched by God. I had to go and I did. Bert was an older, married man with children. He offered to put me up at his house and let me earn my keep. These were still the seventies and getting across the border was simple. Mitch drove us to Buffalo and we got on a plane to California. There were tears, hugs, blessings. I struggled. I had never felt attachment before. It was an odd sensation but we also had a plan that I would return. Mitch, Rider and Gus were the closest thing to a family I had experienced. They loved me, cared for me, protected me, educated me and never once said anything cruel, raised a hand to me or crossed any boundaries. They all slipped me some cash for my trip. I kept my Yonge Street apartment because I would only be gone for a few months. Sometimes the best chance you have for a family is the one you build. It has nothing to do with biology or genetics. Biology is highly over-rated when it comes to defining family. They were good wholesome people, disguised as the devil, to hide, like me, from everyone else. The ink creates a boundary, a bubble. It keeps people away, freaks them out, creates distance."

Chapter Eighteen

Sparta

Come back with your shield—
or on it.
– Plutarch

"May I just begin, Dr. Colby?" I ask.

"If you wish Margaret," he responds.

"The airplane was a new experience for me. I was like a wide-eyed kid tasting ice cream for the first time. Every moment made a permanent impression on me, the stewardesses with their little hats, the seats with the little tray for food, the thick plastic window, the roaring sound of the jet engines, the little air tube above my head blowing in my face, the seat belt tight around my belly, the call button for the stewardess, the carefully choreographed safety demonstration. Then, the highlight of the night, the take off, was amazing. The acceleration, being pushed back in my seat and then leaving the ground, the earth behind, were all astounding sensations. Bert could see my exuberance and he smiled. He was not a person of conversation but he did like to hear himself talk. His temperament was quiet. He spoke through his art and about his art. Bert was a person that spent many hours each day in a state of complete concentration, focussed, obsessed with detail. His art was a solitary activity. Skin was his canvas and Bert Grimm was Da Vinci working on the Mona Lisa creating the most famous smile ever captured. He knew his own brilliance. He was not a modest man. On our flight he told me that he wanted my calf. He wanted that blank canvas of my lower leg to give me a gift, the gift of Grimm."

"We landed at LAX. It was massive. I thought Buffalo was a big airport. Bert's wife and son greeted us and after introductions we were off to Long Beach. Everything in Los Angeles was bigger, the highways, the smell, the cars, even the sun seemed bigger in L.A."

"The Grimm family lived in a modest house near the Nu. Bert could walk to work. I was settled in the guest room and in short order Bert wanted to go to his shop. It was impressive. The front of the shop had a huge sign, Bert Grimm Tattoing and Photos. There was one wall covered in autographed pictures, movie stars, sports stars, musicians. Jack Nicholson, Al Pacino, Paul Newman, John McEnroe,

Magic Johnson, Rickey Henderson, Jeff Beck, David Bowie, all on the wall in poses with Bert. Bert was an orator, a storyteller, each picture had a story. He claimed that in Chicago or St. Louis he had tattooed Bonny and Clyde as well as Pretty Boy Floyd. I was there at the end of the era for Bert, his Nu studio, and his legacy, the late seventies."

"Then there was the art. Catalogues full of drawings sat in the art deco waiting area. It was like Andy Warhol had designed the space. The space itself seemed alive, full of energy, like an affirmative haunting. You could see David Bowie sitting on the leather couch smoking a cigarette, chatting with a young Jack Nicholson. Bert showed me my work area. He refused to allow me to buy my own tools or ink. 'Now,' Bert said, 'give me that calf,' in the most playful way. Bert could read people. In the amusement park, one of the attractions was fortune tellers. Bert was fascinated by this art form and often had his own fortune told. He fancied himself a bit of a psychic."

"I am lying on Bert's table, my calf exposed and he is rubbing it down with alcohol to clean my skin. He says something in a deep monotone voice like, 'you have a warrior in you.' It was scary. I thought he could read my mind. He went on to say, 'this warrior inside you, should be seen outside you and this is my gift to you.' Bert proceeded to ink the most amazing Spartan warrior on my calf. It is beautiful and eerily like Skully in a visual sense. Bert went on to say, 'you were this warrior, in a previous life.' The Spartan had a helmet with the nose plate, a bare chest above rippled abs, a shield battered from conflict, boots to the knee, a leather short/skirt and the short Spartan sword. It took Bert almost two hours to complete the work. In the background, while he worked, his vinyl record played, Led Zepplin,

'Spent my days with a woman unkind, smoked my stuff and drank all my wine.
Made up my mind to make a new start, going to California with an aching in my heart.
Someone told me there's a girl out there with love in her eyes and flowers in her hair.
Took my chances on a big jet plane, never let them tell you that they're all the same.
The sea was red and the sky was grey, wondered how tomorrow

could ever follow today.
The mountains and the canyons started to tremble and shake as the children of the sun began to awake.

Seems that the wrath of the gods
Got a punch on the nose and it started to flow;
I think I might be sinking.
Throw me a line if I reach it in time
I'll meet you up there where the path
Runs straight and high.

To find a queen without a king,
They say she plays guitar and cries and sings... la la la
Ride a white mare in the footsteps of dawn
Tryin' to find a woman who's never, never, never been born.
Standing on a hill in my mountain of dreams,
Telling myself it's not as hard, hard, hard as it seems.'"

"People had gathered in the shop as Bert worked, friends, customers, disciples, the random curious. When he finished Bert helped me up with his hand held high, like he was leading a princess from her throne. He had me stand on the table to model his work. Bert took several pictures of my calf from several angles. It was theatre for those in the shop. Bert went into his speech about Bonny and Clyde, the art of the tattoo, the beauty of ink. It ended with applause. How many people get that response at work? He then had a picture taken of himself standing with me. The pictures were developed in triplicate. Bert signed the picture of him standing with me and gave me a copy. It said, 'to my warrior princess, love Bert'. I packaged up that photograph and mailed it to Mitch, Rider and Gus. I penned a little note and signed it, Love Maggie. I missed my adopted brothers."

"Dr. Colby, some people are just pedestrians in life, putting one foot in front of the other, ever moving forward. They have no passion, no purpose, no life energy. They are a drain on humanity, sucking the life out of others, eating their souls and leaving them for dead. People like my grandfather, my mother, Children's Aid Society are all in that category. Bert Grimm was the opposite end of that spectrum, a positive life force, a spiritual energy, he was on

another plane from most people. He saw the world from a different perspective. Bert Grimm took me under his wing and anointed me into a new world. He was Yoda and I Luke Skywalker."

"I began to work in the Grimm studio. Bert supervised me. His approach was pure Zen, positive, enriching. There was never a negative word, a criticism. He only spoke of what he thought might work and left it to me to decide. He was never imposing, demanding or dogmatic. Bert knew that art came from the soul, it just needed to be discovered and released. I watched him work. He watched me work. He tickled my creative essence and teased it out of me. I learned about colour, texture, depth, shading, perspective. I learned how to be the needle, to be of one mind. He had no agenda to make me a mini-him. Bert wanted my talent, my style, my art to grow out of me as a person. Thus, parallel to my art, I had to come to terms with who I was, as a person. The fundamental question was 'who am I and who am I not'. It was as much spiritual as it was academic."

"I was in Long Beach, California and my world was pretty small considering we were minutes from Los Angeles and Hollywood. Initially I didn't get very far between the shop and Bert's home. I began to explore, as I had in Toronto, walking. Bert never tried to parent me. There were no curfews or rules but he had an enigmatic power. You didn't want to disappoint Bert or let him down in any way. For those reasons you found a self control to respect your love for the man and I did love him. Living in his home, with his family I saw all sides of Bert. He was a beautiful man. Bert had his excesses. He liked to drink from time to time and there was some coke involved, but it did not rule his world in any way."

"The Nu as I explored, I discovered had some fascinating features. The Queen Mary luxury liner was permanently docked there. The Nu had a roller coaster, the Galaxy Steel. The Spruce Goose was near the amusement park in a permanent hanger. My world began to expand as I ventured a little farther each day when I was not in the shop."

"I convinced Bert to take me to a Los Angeles Kings hockey game. They of course were playing the Toronto Maple Leafs. Marcel Dionne was the star of the Kings. Bert loved the hockey, he had never seen a game before."

"One of my new passions was the ocean. It fascinated me. I had never seen one before. The Pacific Ocean held such power, such a majesty. I visited it almost every day. We were so close to it I could hear it at night before I went to sleep. There were things at the ocean beach that I saw as absolute gifts from God, dolphins and surfing. I became obsessed with surfing. The rhythm of it, the sense that you are one with the ocean, part of its power, working in concert with it, excited me the way art and drawing did. I could get lost in it,

shutting out all other thoughts like I did when I worked at the ink."
"I bought a surf board, but I couldn't swim. No one had ever taken me to the YMCA to learn. Undeterred, I signed up for swimming lessons at a local pool. It was an exercise in humility from several perspectives."
"First, there was the bathing suit. For a person covered in tattoos, a bathing suit presents some real challenges. You lose control of who sees your true self. My first day at the pool, I went into the changing room, carrying my little swim bag and almost didn't come out. I went into a little cubicle and put on the suit. Alone in the dressing area, I looked in the mirror and thought, 'hell no'. I wasn't afraid of the water. I wasn't afraid of drowning. I was afraid of being the centre of attention. In a twist of logic I thought my appearance was an advantage because should I sink to the bottom of the pool I would be easily spotted, after all I was primarily blue, not white. These were truly universes colliding, the dark blue underworld of tattoos and the bright white world of swimming. My final challenge was taking off and leaving behind my knife. I had not been without my knife since back in the apartment with Jake when Carolyn taught me how to use it. I was in the change cubical, in the dressing room, staring at my ankle with the knife securely in its sheath. It caused a pause. Bert's voice was in my head, 'life in every breath, baby'. With that mantra, I took off my knife, put it in my bag with my clothes and I walked out onto the pool deck. Boy did the heads turn, there was even some pointing. The pool was a large, Olympic size outdoor pool with a huge, white, cement deck. There were several classes of varying levels going on all at the same time. There was even a spring board diving class underway. I had signed up for an adult beginners swim class, so at least there were no kids in my group staring at me. There were four other people in my class, three men and one other woman. The instructor was quite impressive in his fire engine red Speedo, a full hunk of a man. He introduced himself as Mike and told us all to get into the water. For me, it was one small step for man, one giant leap for mankind. For a moment I felt like a circus sideshow freak exposing my deformity for all to see. Then I said, screw it, we are all in here. I don't care what anyone thinks, I am going to learn to swim, then I am going to learn how to surf. I thought, no one knows me here and I don't care what they think. To cope, I had shut out every-

thing else around me. I shouldn't have. In retrospect I was naïve, Dorothy was no longer in Kansas. The excitement of L.A., the new skills, the new people, seduced me into a false sense of security. I was in L.A., gangs, violence, crime, racial tensions, murders and I was fast asleep, or was I?"

"After three straight days of swimming lessons, my little non-athletic body started to figure out the front crawl. I could get from one side of the pool to the other. This seemed enough to try surfing, after all the surf board is a floatation device; as long as I stay close to it I will be alright. With that, after my day in the tattoo parlour, I was in the water, paddling out to sea. I had watched how it was done. I paddled out, maybe a hundred feet, turned my board around towards the shore and sat on it. Wave after wave went under me and I bobbed up and down like shark bait. It was very hypnotic. I could see other surfers but no one was close to me. Then I realized that just sitting on my board, I was drifting farther and farther out to sea. A little panic set in, but I lie on my board, face down and started paddling back in. Once I did that the waves started to hurl me forward, as they went under me, towards the shore. That first time, I never did try to stand up on my board. I just came to shore with a tremendous thud and a sense of satisfaction. Pulling myself up out of the water I found a spot on the beach and laid down on my towel with my surfboard beside me. It was late evening and I had fallen asleep. It was a deep, but short sleep and I awoke a little disoriented. I wasn't sure where I was. Getting my bearings I realized that it was dark, I was on the beach and I couldn't see anyone else, glancing up and down the beach. A little frenzied I looked and found my swimming bag. My surfboard was beside me and my head was clearing."

"Suddenly I hear a voice from behind me saying, 'I saw you at the swimming pool today.' My instincts kick in and I know this is trouble. People introducing themselves to get acquainted are not standing behind you. Grabbing my bag I turn and see this tubby, short man, holding his dick in his hand. I think, why me, why is it always me? It's Skully time. The little pervert says, 'I am not going to hurt you, just let me finish.' Skully is grinning and responds, 'ya, you are right about one thing, you are not going to hurt me but you are wrong about two other things. First, you are not going to finish and second I am going to hurt you.' That response, the tubby man did not expect. His wiener shrinks and he is tucking himself back in his pants. Skully has this sized up, a quick assessment. He is some pervert, stalker, voyeur, who goes to the pool to stare at young girls and get aroused. Now he has followed me to the beach and has been getting his freak on staring at me while I slept. I missed Skully, her courage, her sense of humour. Skully slowly pulls the knife out of the swimming bag. It is still in its sheath, the leg strap dangling. Carefully she pulls it out, locked in the gaze of the tubby man. It glistens in the moonlight. It feels so good in my hand. Skully lunges forward and draws the knife up from the man's testicles to his stomach, gutting him. He falls forward to his knees then left onto his side. He stares once more at Skully and bleeds out there on the beach. Skully cleans off her blade on the man's shirt and puts the knife away. Looking around she sees no one. We pick up our surfboard, our swimming bag and walk off the beach. I flexed my calf muscle with each step imagining that my Spartan warrior was winking his approval. Walking back to Bert's my thoughts were racing. Bert's voice was in my head, 'who am I and who am I not.' 'Well, Bert,' I am thinking to myself, 'in answer to that question, part of who I am, is a killer. I kill people. That part of myself has a name, Skully. She is my best friend, my protector, my champion.'"

"Dr. Colby? My question for you today is, am I putting myself deliberately at risk? I have reflected a lot on that scene on the beach. From one perspective it is very foolish, very risky, to be on a beach, at night, alone, in L.A. I could also say though, that I accidentally fell asleep and woke up, later than I thought, alone. However, at another level, I know better; intellectually I know that is a stupid thing to do. Am I deliberately putting myself at risk for some reason, perhaps because I want Skully to have to protect me?"

Dr. Colby looks over his glasses, puts down his pad of paper and begins, "Margaret, your story includes a lot of situations where you were victimized. Victimization is powerful, because it means you were powerless. You were powerless to do anything about what was happening to you. You were a child and because there were no adults in your world to step up and protect you, you created Skully. She is your protector, your champion. This should have been an adult, an adult that loved you, unconditionally, but it was not, it was Skully. You, to date, in your story, have not had that person, that protector and you deserved to have that person. Now, more specifically to your question, do you put yourself at risk, on purpose? The short answer Margaret, is yes. When you are abused, victimized as a child, you are fighting forces, battles without weapons. You are a child, not yet fully functioning cognitively, emotionally, socially yet you are being confronted with adult problems. What happens to a child in these circumstances is that they blame themselves. At some level, they think this abuse was their fault. So one of the faulty coping strategies is to put yourself at risk again, to see if you are abused, again, and when it happens, it confirms, in your mind, it was your fault. This creates a significant shift in your psychology. You go from thinking that a bad thing happened to you, to believing that you are bad. This is the shift from guilt to shame."

"Margaret, these things that have happened, your grandfather, your mother, the Switzer's, the kidnapping, the beach, they are not your fault. You created Skully as a way to cope with horrible, stressful, abusive situations. The situations themselves, were not your fault. I know that sounds like psychology mumbo jumbo, but, please, reflect on that, think about it. Skully is part of who you are, not a separate person or personality."

I left Dr. Colby's office, stepped on the elevator and walked through the lobby, holding my breath, holding back tears. My eyes were welling up. In the parking lot I began to weep, uncontrollably. I couldn't do it in front of the doctor. I found a quiet spot around the side of the building and cried. I cried tears of grief. For almost half an hour I wept. I had no thoughts, just tears, sobs. As my thoughts started to gel I realized what I was grieving. I was grieving having not had a father, a protector, a champion, a person who would hold me with unconditional regard. I realized why I was back in Allentown, to find my father, to meet him, to see his face, to hear his story. That was my compulsion. That was the force that drew me back to Allentown. That was the glue that kept me in the shelter, then the hostel. I needed that piece of the story to my life. I know where Dr. Colby was going with his interpretation but what rang loud and clear in my head was, if I had had a dad, none of that would have happened. If I had had a dad, there would be no need for Skully. If I had had a dad he would have protected me, kept me safe and prevented all the violence. I am terrified of men. My grandfather was my first, powerful role model. He was abusive to me in every way possible, physically, sexually, emotionally. As a child I had no coping mechanisms, no defence, no power. I was by the best definition, a victim. I went from my grandfather's care to Jake's care. He too exploited me, physically, sexually, emotionally. Men are like aliens to me. Sick? Twisted?

Chapter Nineteen

The Sperm Donor

Men are generally more careful of the breed of their horses and dogs than of their children.
– William Penn

Back in the hostel I have new purpose. I am going to find my father. I have figured it out. This loose end to my life is what has compelled me to stay in Allentown. I am trying to be realistic about what I may find. It could very well be some loser my mother met and had a one night stand with. He may not even know that I exist. However, none the less, the questions need to be answered. It is at the level of obsession. These thoughts consume me and I cannot change the channel. It is like a record with a scratch, forever skipping back to the same place and replaying the same lyrics. Finding my father is a huge challenge because I don't even know his name. My mother is dead, so she can't help me. Desperate times call for desperate measures; I am going to ask for help.

The chaplain at the Salvation Army Hostel is a soft, placid man of God. He makes me sick. However, I am thinking that he will help me. He is a tall, thin man with a gentle face. Approaching his office in the hostel I feel creepy. It's all the crosses, pictures of Christ, the candles, they bother me. Knocking on the door I have rehearsed my speech several times. My cue to cry is, 'I never knew my father'. Reverend Phil has a lovely office with a couch, chair and coffee table, a large desk, a bookcase full to overflowing with books and a long credenza covered with framed photographs of people. We sit in his little meeting area, I on the couch, he in his well-worn, somewhat out of place chair. The chair is much older than all the other furniture, worn, like it came from another time and place. I assumed it was his chair.

I begin our conversation, "Reverend Phil?"

He responds, "Please Margaret, no titles here, I am happy with just Phil."

Smiling I continue, "Phil, I need someone's help."

He returns the smile, "Yes of course Margaret, what can I do for you?"

With permission I say, "I would like to find my father, or at least find out about him. I have never met him. I don't even know his name."

Reverend Phil, surprisingly confident, says, "I can help you with that. Your full name is Margaret Anne Sellars, right?"

A little shocked he knows that, I lower my eyes to the floor and say, "Yes, sir. It is."

Phil replies, "Good, that's all I need. We bible thumper types stick together. You were born here in Allentown, right? I can call the pastor at the hospital and he can search your name in their electronic records. When a child is born it is a requirement that a father be named on the Record of Live Birth. Let's start there. Your mother may have given a false name, but maybe not."

That was easy. I didn't have to cry or beg or even appear pathetic, after all. The reverend is up and behind his desk on the phone. The bible on the coffee table in front of me catches my eye. It is beautiful, leather bound with a yellow silk book mark hanging out of it. I dare not touch it in case it bursts into flames in my hands. I can hear Phil on the phone, "Jack you old dog, can you do me a favour? Do you have your computer on there? Search the name Margaret Anne Sellars and tell me what pops up." There is a short pause and I hear Phil say, "Great! Is there a father's name on that file? Jacob William Hammel? Date of birth, February 22, 1942. Can you fax that over to me please? Thanks Jack, I owe you one. Let's get a lunch, maybe a round of golf."

Stunned, I am speechless. That was so easy. I thought it would take weeks of searching and perhaps a private detective to get that name. Reverend Phil writes the name and birth date on a piece of paper and gives it to me as easy as that. He must see my disbelief and he says, "God works in mysterious ways my child but computers, they are the bomb. Bless you. And if I can be of any further assistance don't hesitate to come back."

Walking out of the reverend's office with my father's name in my hand, I am crying again. That's twice today with the tears. I must be on to something because I don't cry.

Putting myself together I am heading for the common room of the hostel. It is a leisure area with ping-pong, pool, cards and internet access. I have letter recognition skills but no real reading ability, so I type in the name, Jacob William Hammel and hit enter. I grab one of the other residents and tell them I can't find my glasses and ask them to read the search results. Three hits pop up, all impossible in terms of being my dad. One notation was for a Swedish Evangelical minister, can't be dad. So, moving on to easy plans, I ask my literate friend to go to Canada 411 and type in the name, nothing. That exhausts my easy search options, I am discouraged. My options are exhausted and so am I. I go to my cot and lay down falling into a deep sleep.

Chapter Twenty

Surf and Turf

Surfing is very much like making love.
It always feels good, no matter how many times you've done it.
– Paul Strauch

I outlined to Dr. Colby my progress in finding my father. He was very cautious, "Please be careful Margaret. I have seen this dynamic before and it can be very explosive. You have so many suppressed feelings about your past, including your father, this could really blow the lid off of Pandora's Box and send you into a real tailspin. I am going to give you my emergency phone number. It's a cell. If this blows up, I need you to promise you will call me immediately. I promise that I will drop whatever I am doing and meet you."

Perplexed, I say, "OK, but I think I am being realistic."

Dr. Colby replies, "So did the captain of the Titanic."

I respond, "OK, I get you. I will call if it all goes badly. I am still no closer to actually finding him though."

The doctor, for emphasis, adds, "Please, be careful, you are playing with fire here. Can we pick up your story in California?"

Jumping in I say, "The days are moving forward. I finished the swimming lessons. I was officially a 'guppy'. I was up on my surfboard, well, up and down, maybe more down than up, but I loved it."

"One morning I got up early to surf and upon returning to Bert's shop, entering the door, there was a cop sitting in the waiting area. Bert was chatting him up and as I entered they both stood up. I am searching Bert's face for some clue as to what is going on. I am wearing my best poker face. Bert seems sad, worried, not alarmed, so I offer the, 'what's up?', introduction. Bert walks to me and asks me to sit down. I do."

"Bert says, 'Margaret, your mother is dead.'"

"The officer jumps in, 'I am sorry Margaret, the Canadian authorities contacted us. There is no easy way to say this, your mother was murdered. Your stepmother, Ellen, helped the Canadian police find their way to Mitch in Toronto and Mitch said you were here with Bert. Now, that all took several weeks, so your mom has already been buried. I am sorry, but we have other problems that you need to be aware of. Your mom was involved in trafficking drugs and gambling. The Canadian authorities are investigating a triple homicide related to the gambling ring. They are assuming that your mother was killed because of her gambling debts, but there are also some drug people, some very bad people, looking for some missing money that also relates somehow to your mom. Ellen, your stepmother, says that you ran away, is that true Margaret? There is also a worry that when you ran away, you took some drug money with you, is that possible Margaret?'"

"Dr. Colby, I was trying to look calm but my heart was beating out of my chest. I quietly agreed, 'yes, I ran away.' 'No, I didn't take any drug money.' I learned a long time ago to give the shortest answer possible so as not to build a web of lies you can't remember later."

"I couldn't figure out how anyone would have gotten from the van with the Three dead Stooges to Mitch in Toronto. That's some serious Sherlock Holmes detective work there. 'How?' I am terrified at that moment thinking I am going to be deported, or arrested, something."

"The policeman says, 'OK', we all know Bert here in Long Beach and he has vouched for you. You are here as his guest, staying in his house, so it's all good. I am sorry for your loss Margaret, but it is better that you know. Ellen, your stepmother would like to hear from you, so here is her number, and I believe there are some things for you back in Allentown that belonged to your mom as well as some money from the estate. Again, I am sorry for your loss, good-bye. Oh, and by the way Margaret, if you have the drug money, or even if you don't have it but the drug people think you do, keep your head up. These are cruel, relentless people." And with that the officer leaves.

"Bert looks at me and says, 'Baby, it's all good. I love you and you don't have to say anything or do anything. I don't need to know anything. You just need to recognize that I am here for you, my family is here for you and whatever you need, you just ask for it. If you need some time, some space, some drugs .... Just kidding. Whatever you need baby, we are here for you.'"

"I looked at Bert and said, 'I would like to surf.'"
"He smiled and said, 'I want to see that.'"
"We went to the beach, surfed, laughed, ate, laid in the California sun. Bert brought his ghetto blaster and we listened to Cat Stevens,

'Now that I've lost everything to you,
you say you want to start something new,
and it's breaking my heart you're leaving,
baby I'm grieving.

But if you wanna leave take good care,
hope you have a lot of nice things to wear,
but then a lot of nice things turn bad out there.
Oh baby baby it's a wild world,
it's hard to get by just upon a smile.
Oh baby baby it's a wild world.

I'll always remember you like a child, girl.
You know I've seen a lot of what the world can do,
and it's breaking my heart in two,
'cause I never want to see you sad girl,
don't be a bad girl,
but if you wanna leave take good care,
hope you make a lot of nice friends out there,
but just remember there's a lot of bad and beware,
beware,

Oh baby baby it's a wild world,
it's hard to get by just upon a smile
Oh baby baby it's a wild world,
and I'll always remember you like a child, girl.'"

"As we lay there in the sand, with the sun setting, in a moment of peace and serenity that I will never forget, Bert said, 'I have a gift for you Maggie. I am an artist, but I am also a businessman. I have for you, a million dollar idea. This will make you rich. I have no doubt in my mind, this will make you rich. You are talented beyond belief, the best I have ever worked with. Your talent goes beyond, way beyond the world of tattoos. You are an artist in the purest sense of the word. Your talent is under appreciated here in the world of tattoos. It is my honour to know you. Some people love the ink and they can do a good tat, but you are out there in another stratosphere. You have an incredible future tattooing and I know you will never stop now. However, when I look at you and your love for surfing, the sea, I see another possibility. The board, this big long board, is just another canvas. Airbrushing and tattooing are the same skill. If you took this board and painted it, with your designs, you would be rich. Now baby, I have already taken the liberty of using my vast network and I have found a surfboard manufacturer, here in Long Beach. I have talked to them, they know me, and they are flipped out about this idea. These guys custom build boards for the best surfers in the world. They are wealthy, crazy, funky people and you my dear, could blow their minds with your work. I am giving you this gift because I love you, I believe in you and you deserve this. You are not a kid anymore, baby, you are here, you are with me and I am telling you, you are ready to conquer the world. It's up to you. You don't have to decide right now. It's been a big day. Take your time. I love you.'"

"With that, Bert got up, kissed me on top of the head and said, 'I will see you at home.'"

"Bert had a flare for the dramatic. He must have been waiting for the right moment to say all that. He was an amazing, gifted man."

Dr. Colby interjects, "Did you ever figure out how the authorities found you?"

I pause, and upset I offer, "Yes, I figured it out. My curiosity got the better of me and I had to call Ellen. I had to find out what she had for me, from my mother. My mother had never given me anything, no birthday presents, no Christmas presents, no puppies, nothing. So, yes, I was curious when I heard my mother had left me something. I asked Bert and he allowed me to use his phone at home. I called Ellen. This is a story, within a story. The short answer to how the authorities found me is that Ellen found me."

"My mom was killed shortly after I took off with the drug money. Initially, when they, my mom and Ellen, thought that I had run away, Ellen filed a missing persons report. I know my mom would not have thought of that or cared enough to do that. After my mom passed Ellen went even farther. She went on a mission to find me. She started locally, with posters, flyers, like I was a lost cat. Then she broadened her search. One of her strategies, because so many kids run to Toronto, was to go to Toronto, Yonge Street. Ellen went to Yonge Street and started handing out flyers with my picture on it. It took several weekends but eventually someone tied me to the tattoo parlour. Ellen was Sherlock Holmes. Ellen told the police and the police did the rest. Mitch, Rider and Gus would have tried to protect my anonymity but I am sure they could be intimidated into giving me up or they could have felt sympathy for my mom's passing and thought I would want to know. Regardless, bingo, I am found."

"When I am on the phone with Ellen, she also says that she and the lawyers she works for, have dealt with my mother's affairs, sold the house, closed out her bank account and put everything in an interest bearing trust account for me. Ellen said there was one hundred and twenty-five thousand dollars, being held in trust for me. I asked about mother's gambling and her debts. Ellen said that the house had appreciated in value, significantly and mother's little business had done well. She said everything was free and clear."

"Ellen said there were some personal things of my mom's that she was holding on my behalf. Ellen said that she would like me to come and live with her. I explained a little bit about the tattooing and surfing and that at that time, I didn't see myself back in Allentown."

"The trust fund idea fascinated me. I asked Ellen if I or someone else could contribute to the fund and make it grow. She said yes."

"I liked Bert's idea about airbrushing surfboards but I didn't know about being legitimate, having a profile, a bank account, a business. With my past and certain events, acts, I needed to fly under the radar, off the grid. All the money in the world isn't worth life in prison. Being found by the police scared the life out of me."

"I developed this system to hide, launder, money, cash. Bert, who I trusted with my life, agreed to take money from me, cash and in his name, contribute to the trust fund. He would send cheques, under his name, to the account in Canada. To test the system I started by sending twenty thousand dollars through Bert to the trust account. This was a portion of the drug money I took from my mother. Bert, as the depositor was entitled to a receipt confirming the trust account existed. It worked! Bert received a statement from the lawyer, Ellen's boss, showing the account, in my name, confirming the deposit. I also had my statements sent to Bert's shop. It all worked."

"For this to work, in my business, I had to accept payment in cash only, for my work. The surfer dudes were cool with that plan and I started a cash business, a lot of cash. It wasn't that different from the tattoo business. It too was primarily a cash business."

"I was working one day a week with Bert and the rest of the week with the surfer dudes. I met some of the greats in surfing, Rabbit Bartholemew, Ben Aipa, Buttons and Dane Kealoha, Larry Bertleman. I sold them and their manufacturers artwork for surfboards. It was straight up cash sales like a rapper today would buy a rhyme. I had no interest in having my name on a surfboard or a company. I simply inscribed my initials on the art work. Bret was smart enough to help me create a royalties agreement and flowed all the cash to Bert, and Bert sent it on to the trust account. I kept a small slush fund for myself to live off of, but by and large the money went to trust. The account grew and grew; by the time I was twenty, I had over half a million dollars. Bert was right. It was a million dollar idea. My original three month plan for California turned into about two years. Probably the best two years of my life, working the ink, surfing, the surfboard guys. I had a side trip to Hawaii, on surfing business. I went to the famous RV's Ocean Sports Surf Shop and met the famous Uncle Roy, Roy Vierra."

"Dr. Colby, I didn't think a lot about money. I didn't tediously review each trust account statement to see if I was getting an appropriate interest rate on my principal amount. I was happy to have a group of people around me that cared about me, that looked out for me. I was happy to be doing what I loved, art, to be surfing."

Dr. Colby interrupts, "So, you are twenty, somewhat wealthy, and here you are today, homeless and destitute. I have to ask, what happened?"

I end with, "A story for another day Dr. Colby, our time is up."

Chapter Twenty-one

Betrayal

We have to distrust each other.
It is our only defence against
betrayal.
– Tennessee Williams

I am enjoying keeping Dr. Colby in suspense. Once again in his comfortable office chair I am deep in my story, "After two years in California I returned to Toronto. Mitch, Rider and Gus welcomed me home with open arms. They had helped me keep my apartment. We had a wonderful reunion with hugs, kisses, dinner and tales of my adventures in California. The lads couldn't believe how much I had grown up, matured. It was all so great, that feeling of family. My return had been advertised from a business perspective and I was back in the Tattoo You shop, a celebrity, having worked with Bert Grimm. I had a waiting list of customers. My life back in Toronto was very modest considering my assets. Aided by the exchange rate between the United States and Canada, I was doing exceptionally well, with royalty amounts being flowed through Bert and his family to the trust account. It worked amazingly. Even in Toronto I could do original designs, send them to California and sell them through Bert's shop. I had told Mitch, Rider and Gus of my success but not in pure numerical, financial terms. They didn't care about bank accounts. They were happy, that I was happy."

"A great deal about myself had changed. As my world expanded so did my skills. I was more confident, articulate, outgoing. I still looked like an urchin, a freak, a street person but I was no longer that person. I had some life experience that had educated me. I was not book smart but I was a quick study. I had a certain business sense to go with my street smarts. My street smarts had helped me develop a solid business acumen. My ability to read people had guided me to places where not only had I profited but others had profited too. I had developed a network of people that I could trust and they believed in me, relied on me. There were people in my corner now. I didn't feel so all alone any more. It was a good feeling."

"I had it in my head, there in the early 80's, past my twentieth birthday, that I needed to legitimize myself, somehow. There were things that I wanted. I wanted to drive, to own a car, perhaps a small house. I wanted a passport, to travel, surf."

"To start, during our reunion, I discussed, with Mitch, Rider and Gus the idea of opening a new shop, a partnership. I had some ideas about new revenue streams, new revenue streams that respected the art. My buy in price to their business was to pay for the new shop. We were going to be full and equal partners. I would front all the money to lease, renovate and outfit the new shop. The boys were thrilled and it was all done on a handshake."

"We decided to go to Allentown, to visit Ellen and my lawyer, Mr. Spitz and see what my options were. I thought a lawyer could make me legitimate, get me a birth certificate, a social insurance number, a life."

"Mitch drove us all to Allentown, he had a licence. I rented us a car. We had arranged to meet Ellen at her apartment. It was an exciting drive, a true road trip, an adventure. We were discussing the new shop, new ventures, a new life. There was such a strong, positive energy."

"I was actually looking forward to seeing Ellen again. She had been kind to me, while I lived with her and my mother. Ellen had some parenting instincts, skills. She had come from a strong family and received a formal college education."

"I created for myself a vision of our reunion. There was me the long lost daughter, reuniting with her stepmother after years of being away. There would be hugs and tears. However, Ellen, when we met her, did not have the reaction of a stepmother seeing her stepdaughter after almost three years. She seemed anxious, almost scared. The words were all correct, she said the right things, but the facial expressions, the body language didn't match. The wrinkles between the eyes, the tight mouth, the choppy sentences were all a dead giveaway, something was wrong. Mitch saw it, something was not quite right with Ellen and our reunion. We exchanged some glances to confirm that we were reading the same signals. Rider was so excited he was oblivious. Gus was always a little slow on the uptake but I could tell he had seen it too. Something was off beam."

"I told Ellen that I would like to transfer two hundred and fifty thousand dollars from my trust account to Mitch so I could buy into their business, be a partner. According to my trust account statements, that was less than a third of what was in my account. That was my buy in price to Tattoo You. Ellen said that we had to go to the lawyer's office to address the paper work."

"It was a tense, quiet ride over to the lawyer's office. The lawyer that Ellen worked for was David Spitz. He was managing my trust account and forwarding me financial statements. He greeted us as we entered his office building saying he would be with us momentarily as he sat us in his board room. Mr. Spitz was in his early forties, fit, with brown hair, brown eyes. He had an endearing smile and at just over six feet tall it would have been easy to describe him as handsome. In fact he was one of the beautiful people, too handsome, too charming. He was in a law practice by himself working out of an old downtown two story house. It was a beautiful office building with stained glass windows, ornate wood work, hardwood floors and frosted glass in the doors. Ellen offered us coffee in his conference room around a huge dark walnut boardroom table. The walls were covered in original artwork, sculptures sat on the side tables. We must have looked pretty out of place there, these four tattooed people, with our grubby clothes, unkempt appearance. We looked more like vagrants than business partners. There was more money in decorations and art in that room than I would see in three life times."

"Mr. Spitz came in, he was carrying a file and he sat at the head of the table. His sharply cut suit hung on him like he had just stepped out of a GQ magazine. He was smiling, at first, then there was a strange silence, his presentation changed, dramatically. Mitch, Rider, Gus and I were exchanging glances, puzzled glances. Mr. Spitz was distressed, upset in an angry aggressive manner. He launched into a tirade that started with, 'You stole from me.'"

"My heart was in my throat. I was speechless, but 'What are you talking about?' spilled out of me."

"The lawyer offers, 'OK, I am going to explain, straight to the point. The little enterprise that your mother was in, the drugs, I was the money, the bank. When you walked off with that thirty thousand dollars, that was my thirty thousand dollars, my money. I held your mother responsible for that money. She thought she could recover the money, replace it. I was nice. I gave her time, a chance, but her misadventures with gambling got her killed before I got my money. Again, I was nice, I settled your mother's estate, set up the trust fund, took my thirty grand out of the estate and thought we were settled, and we were. I was going to leave the money alone, in your trust, and let the interest accumulate for you. My intentions were good, but, in the end, I am a crooked lawyer, financing drug deals, living off my clients' trust money. When more money started arriving to the account, I couldn't resist. Have you ever heard of a Ponzi scheme? The bottom line is, I have been living off of your trust account and the trust accounts of other clients and living quite well I might add. It was a good idea, in fact it was a great idea, but you have created a real problem. You have asked for more money than is currently in the account. So, my dear, the jig is up, you have caught me with my pants down, exposed. If you had asked for fifty grand, I would have given it to you, but we have a situation here. I don't have the two hundred and fifty thousand dollars you have asked to withdraw from your trust account.'"

"There was a long pause and he continued, 'Look, this is what I am thinking, you, Margaret, you are no one, you don't really even exist. I don't think you can go to the cops or the Law Society and rat me out. I think you will end up in more trouble than I ever could by making a stink and going to the authorities. I think that because I know a crooked deal when I see one. It's that old don't bullshit a bullshitter situation. The cheques from Bert Grimm, that's you laundering money, isn't it? Don't answer, that's a rhetorical question. I know the answer. There is a list of other reasons why you won't turn me in. Let's try immigration issues. We could go to income tax evasion. Not happy yet? Let's try working in the United States without a green card. You could take a shot at me, by calling the police, but I am betting that from my law office, I could bring down you, Bert Grimm and these three thugs that you have with you today. I could crush all of you. So here is what we are going to do. I am going to give you fifty grand, and we are going to call it even, done, square, over. I shouldn't give you anything, but, I am going to be nice, out of respect for your mother and our former, profitable business arrangement.' With that he opened up his file and gave me a certified cheque for fifty thousand dollars, payable to me, no one."

"I was furious, Dr. Colby, enraged, Skully was taking over and I could feel her reaching for the knife. I thought my head was going to explode. I could feel myself physically heating up. My fists were clenched. Skully was going to kill the lawyer, then Ellen, right there in that beautiful, plush, richly decorated office."

"Then, for the first time, ever, I controlled Skully, she didn't override me. I couldn't let that happen in front of Mitch, Rider and Gus. I boiled. I had just lost something shy of one million dollars. My dream of being partners with the lads was shattered. Mitch, Rider and Gus almost had to carry me out of the office. They were confused but they got the essence of what just happened. I just got screwed, burned."

"It's funny how in one moment your greatest weakness can become your greatest strength. The lawyer was right. I was no one. I was no one, with nothing to lose."

"I convinced the lads, Mitch, Rider and Gus that I would be fine and that they should drive back to Toronto and leave me in Allentown. I persuaded them that I could straighten this all out. They reluctantly left me behind. I went straight back to Ellen's apartment and waited for her to return. Ellen had no idea who she was dealing with. I am sure, in her mind I was just a teenager, a runaway, a foster child, who took off with more money than I had ever seen before. When she came home she took me into her apartment, willingly, blinded by guilt. I was giving her my pathetic victim look. She fucked my mother, then she fucked me. She was apologizing, saying she had no choice. Ellen was shaking, literally, her hands rattled, the reality of her complicit role in the theft from my trust fund was catching up to her. Ellen was a good person, with strong values, she felt guilt, unlike her boss the lawyer. This was going to be my first true murder, planned, premeditated. I knew exactly what I was going to do, while I waited for Ellen to come home. I thought it through, fantasized about it. This was not a reactionary, self-defence killing. I thought this one through in detail. Then, having talked my way into the apartment I was standing behind Ellen, my knife at her throat, telling her to write down the lawyer's home address. After her complete compliance I drew my razor sharp knife across her throat, crossing her carotid artery. I watched her die on her kitchen floor. Carefully, slowly, I looted her apartment, taking a gym bag full of jewellery, money and the envelope from my mother marked, 'Margaret'. With the gym bag over my shoulder I walked back to the lawyer's office. It was after hours now, dark and I carefully scoped out the office, walking the full perimeter of the building, several times. I wanted him to be alone and he was. I could see David Spitz, the lawyer sitting at his desk. He had a bottle of Scotch on his bureau, with a lovely crystal four ounce glass on a ceramic coaster. Cleary he was celebrating his success, pleased with himself. He had just screwed a little girl out of just under one million dollars. I could have broken in, quietly and stabbed him to death but this situation called for more. I knocked on the front door."

"The lawyer, in his arrogance, came to the door, with his crystal four ounce glass of Scotch in his right hand. He let me in without so much as a question or hesitation. The lawyer had underestimated me. I knew how he saw me, as a helpless, vulnerable, weak little girl. After all, I was physically tiny, deformed by years of neglect, malnutrition, tattoos and my nervous tic of pulling out my own hair. At the door to his office I was the picture of innocence, helpless, hopeless. I wanted this killing to be worthy, a worthy execution. It was going to be beautiful."

"Circling the office I had time to plan, fantasize. In his office I wanted to make him vulnerable and I was going to use my sexuality to do it, to make him susceptible, unaware, after all I had worked as a prostitute. Men are so stupid, their egos, their naive sense of sexuality."

"In his office, I was standing across from him. He was behind his desk, I in front of the desk. He looked so smug, so confident, pleased with himself. Slowly, seductively I took off my shirt. There were no words spoken. He swung his chair to one side and slouched down slightly so as to hang his junk off the edge of his chair. I could hear him pulling down his fly opening up his pants. Moving around the desk I kneeled in front him. I reached out with one hand and grabbed his chubbed penis, with the other hand I pulled out my knife. With one slash I cut off his dick. Standing up I dropped the loose flesh into his four ounce crystal glass of Scotch. He was quickly going into shock, shaking he fell on the floor. It looked like it hurt like hell. I jumped on top of him with my knees on either side of his head and I sat on his chest. I dug my knife in his mouth and I cut out his tongue. Hopping up, I added that flesh to his crystal four ounce glass of Scotch. Turning around I stepped on his wrist, kneeling over I cut off the index finger of his right hand. I put that too in his crystal four ounce glass of Scotch. He was choking on the blood in his mouth. I wasn't ready for him to die so I rolled him over on his stomach. I pulled down his pants to his ankles, then his baby blue silk boxer underwear. With one foot on his back I bent over and cut off his testicles. I put them in the crystal four ounce glass of Scotch, Scotch on the rocks. There were still no words spoken. I rolled him over again and slashing, I disfigured his handsome face. He was not dead yet. I was in no hurry. He was moaning, breathing. I wanted him to suffer. I wanted to see him suffer. I sat on his desk, beside his four ounce crystal glass of Scotch on the rocks and I watched him die, slowly on the floor behind his desk. His breath got shallow, his eyes rolled up into his head. It was beautiful. He had fucked with the wrong little girl. He was motionless on the floor, dead."

"I had a long hot shower in his en suite bathroom and changed into clothes that I had taken from Ellen's. I knew, because he was nothing more than an overdressed drug dealer that he would have cash on hand and drugs. I searched his office, top to bottom. In his file storage room I found a bankers box full of cash behind a row of filing cabinets. In his law library I found cocaine, hidden behind books of justice. I emptied the wrapped bills into my gym bag. Then I added his jewellery, watch, tie clip, rings. Back in his office I set up a little cocaine scene beside his crystal four ounce glass of Scotch on the rocks. I left the remainder of the cocaine in his desk. I thought that should cover my tracks. I had found his ring of keys. Stepping out the back door of his office I pulled out the piece of paper with his home address on it. Walking to his house I felt the weight of my night's work in the gym bag over my shoulder."

"The house was magnificent, a Tudor style mansion, surrounded by an iron fence. When I searched his office I could find no evidence of family, no pictures of a wife or children. He was too narcissistic to have a family. It was clear to me that life was all about him, David Spitz, the lawyer. I crawled under the front gate and ran to the back of the house, and hiding my gym bag I let myself quietly in the back door. My target, again, was cash, jewellery. I found a large kit bag in his walk-in closet off of his overdone bedroom. Carefully, methodically I went through every room of the house. He had quite the collection of coins, watches, tie clips, cuff links and of course more cash. I knew when he said he couldn't afford to pay out the money I had requested, he was lying. He had lots of money, more money than brains. I didn't count the money I collected out of his house or his office. Taking the two bags over my shoulders I walked through his backyard, through his neighbours yard and out onto the street behind his. I walked to downtown Allentown and got on a Greyhound bus back to Toronto."

"Back in my Toronto apartment I fell into a deep fitful sleep. I was exhausted with a bag full of loot on either side of myself as I slept. I awoke to the sound of knocking on my door. It was Mitch calling out my name. I crawled out of bed and opened the door. Seeing it was truly Mitch I passed out in his arms. More than passed out, I blacked out. Later, I learned from Mitch that I sort of melted into the floor, crying, babbling."

"That initiated my first mental health stay in hospital. I awoke in a hospital bed on the adult mental health inpatient unit at Toronto Memorial Hospital. When I woke up Mitch was at my bedside, apologizing. He didn't know what to do when he found me in such a messed up state. I was incoherent, babbling nonsense. He took me to the hospital. Mitch said that I had a nervous breakdown. I was out of it. My memory was really vague, and still is, but I know that Mitch had taken the bags of money and loot out of my apartment. I knew that I could trust him. He had called Bert and the cheques for the trust fund were re-directed, to an account Mitch set up, payable to him. Money was still flowing in. Mitch kept the little enterprise alive by sending work he had in his shop that I had done, to California."

"Six months, Dr. Colby, I was in the hospital for six months. At least one of my group of friends, Mitch, Rider and Gus visited me almost every day. We did not speak about what happened in Allentown. They knew and they knew that I knew they knew. Mitch, Rider and Gus all have their own histories, their own stories. They were not public school teachers. They were people from the street, like me. They knew the code of the street, never rat."

"They brought in pictures of the new tattoo parlour, as it was being built, right on Yonge Street, exactly as we had planned. From the hospital I was never sure I would see it or ever work in it. I was a mental health patient now. I functioned in a zombie-like state, shuffling the hospital hallways in my hospital gown, eyes sunken, unable to focus, drooling. I was diagnosed with depression and schizophrenia. Now, I was sedated, drugged with anti-psychotic and depression medication. I was told by the nursing staff that when I was admitted, I was completely out of it. I was talking to Skully, she was talking to me. The doctors thought I was delusional. One of the nurses told me that I aggressed towards the psychiatrist, attacked him, during the assessment reaching for my knife and that got me placed on the secure unit, the locked unit. Trapped, caged, I attempted suicide by slashing my wrists with a pair of scissors I stole from the nurse's station. It was at this time I received Electro Convulsive Therapy. Now, I could not leave the hospital without a doctor discharging me, no more running."

"Dr. Colby, I was really screwed up at that point. I had been betrayed by my mother, my stepmother, my lawyer. It was such a fall, a complete hard drive crash. I had been doing so well. I had friends, an income, an occupation, a hobby, even a future and it all fell apart like a house of cards. I should have known it was too good to be true. I was trailer park trash. I wasn't a businesswoman, an artist or an entrepreneur. I was nobody, exactly as the crooked lawyer described me. Life only lets me get so far then it pulls the rug right out from under my feet. I can't succeed. I can't get ahead. I can't go legit. I am predisposed to be a complete fuck up, a failure. I can't dig myself out of it. Here I am, again, in your office, homeless, destitute, thinking if I could find my father I could … no, I can't. There is always something missing, some piece I can't find that would make the puzzle complete, fill in my emptiness. I always have a blind spot, something that is there, in front of me, that I can't see. It is a form of denial, demons that haunt me. Sometimes, I feel so close to being complete, whole, then, bang, I crash and burn. This time I am convinced that it is my father. I need that piece of the puzzle, then I believe that I can rebuild, again. There are a huge number of stories yet to be told, stories about the six months in hospital, my discharge and life after that first hospitalization. I was just past twenty years old when that happened, now I am forty-six, I think."

"Do you know what keeps me going Dr. Colby? Suicide! I am ready, willing and able to kill myself. That is my shield. Somewhere along the line I decided, if I am willing to kill myself, why not live a life of adventure first. When you are resigned to the idea of suicide, you lose all fear. You don't care about things like money, food, people, or family. You are prepared to sacrifice it all. I don't care if I live or die anyway. If someone, or something were to kill me, I would thank them. I welcome death. It will be a release from this torment. So, I am on an adventure, an adventure to find my father."

 Dr. Colby looks pensive. I have confessed to being a murderous, homicidal, suicidal, maniac. I am guessing but I think he is worried about his own safety. From time to time I catch him glancing at my ankles to see if my knife is there and it is. I could easily be diagnosed as a sociopath, but the problem is time. What I have confessed to him occurred twenty plus years ago but it could still put me in jail. It is not, perhaps, in his mind a reflection of today. I have kept today, recent events by and large, secret.

 I rescue the good doctor and say, "I know, our time is up, I will see you next week." Waiting at the elevator outside Dr. Colby's office I hear music. It is Bob Dylan,

'I am a lonesome hobo
Without family or friends,
Where another man's life might begin,
That's exactly where mine ends.
I have tried my hand at bribery,
Blackmail and deceit,
And I've served time for ev'rything
'Cept beggin' on the street.
Well, once I was rather prosperous,
There was nothing I did lack.
I had fourteen-karat gold in my mouth
And silk upon my back.
But I did not trust my brother,
I carried him to blame,
Which led me to my fatal doom,
To wander off in shame.
Kind ladies and kind gentlemen,
Soon I will be gone,
But let me just warn you all,
Before I do pass on;
Stay free from petty jealousies,
Live by no man's code,
And hold your judgment for yourself
Lest you wind up on this road.'

Chapter Twenty-two

Searching

As I walk back to the hostel and turn the corner, for the second time in my recent past, I see police cars in front of my place of residence. There are no other emergency vehicles and there are no lights flashing so I assume this is not a tragedy unfolding. At this point in my life, deep in my suicidal ideation, I don't care if they are there for me. I have no anxiety seeing the police cars. What ever happens, happens, is my attitude at this point in time. Entering the automatic sliding front door I see the familiar face of Constable Kane. He is sitting in the waiting area of the Salvation Army Hostel looking around at the posters on the wall. Spotting me, and showing quite a good memory he hails me over with, "Margaret."

Moving towards him I show an equally good recall with, "Constable Kane."

He engages me with, "Hey, sorry about the thing at the shelter. I didn't mean to accuse you of helping that crazy husband get in the shelter. That investigation has been closed. He blew himself up and almost everyone else, with the truck bomb. It is still a funny story. Apparently he shopped for a week to find the right dress. It of course had nothing to do with you. I am glad you are OK."

It doesn't take a woman long to figure out when a man's interest has an overly intense sexual component. The excessively erect posture; chest out; the fixed eyes on the breasts; the swelling lips; the deeper voice; are all clear signals that we are not just passing time. I conclude that young Constable Kane has a less than professional interest in me. I know that he has read my file, my record, from our last encounter. It is not a stretch to think that he knows my history includes prostitution. Men, sexually suppressed, inexperienced men are fascinated with prostitution. They watch pornography and think that it is real sex. Their wild imaginations and a bar of soap are enough to send them into a sexual frenzy as they fantasize about what a professional sex partner would do to them. Constable Kane is in a lather.

As I approach the good constable I put this together with my need to find a certain Jacob William Hammel, my father and I see a possible solution. My own efforts are at a standstill, after Google, I got nothing.

I offer, "Constable Kane, what are you doing here?"

He replies, "We are just dropping off a new customer for you. We found him asleep in an alley downtown. So, you know, We Serve and Protect."

This little exchange, in my mind, is flirting. It is certainly not police work. He is out of bounds.

I love a good game, "Do you want to serve and protect me, Constable Kane?"

"Why yes of course ma'am. I would be happy to serve a damsel in distress. What can I do for you?" he replies.

"Can we go somewhere a little more private and talk?" I ask.

"Certainly, where do you suggest?" he enquires.

"There is a family meeting room just down the hall. We could go there," I suggest.

"Lead, and I shall follow. I am at your service," he responds, promptly.

Walking down the rather institutional hallway I am considering my options. I am hoping that my good Constable Kane will use his magic computer in his patrol car and search the name of one Jacob William Hammel.

In the quiet family meeting room I sit too close to the constable on the leather couch, in his personal space, to see his reaction. He does not move away or push me away. We are on the same page. I begin with, "Do you have a first name Constable Kane?"

He answers, voice cracking, "Jim, my first name is Jim."

"Jim," I begin, "I have a problem. I am an orphan. My mother has passed away, my grandfather that raised me has also passed. I have no brothers or sisters and I never knew my father. I have never met him, seen a picture of him or heard from him in any way. I am here, in this hostel, struggling, looking for supports. Do you think, with your incredible detective skills that you could help me find him?" I ask.

He seems reluctantly perplexed, so I decide to give him a partner in crime. I explain to Jim, "The chaplain here, Father Phil, he was able to get a search of my hospital birth record. He got me a full name and a birthdate." Now, I know, and Constable Kane knows and Father Phil knows, he should not have done that. Father Phil has accessed and released confidential information on my behalf. I offer this to help Constable Kane make the wrong decision too, and he does.

He says, "OK, give me the name and the birthdate and I will do a CPIC search. If he has a criminal record he will show up or even if he has a drivers licence, his name will pop up, that should at least give you an address to start. But I can't do that right now. Write down the information and I will look it up."

Being illiterate is such a nuisance some times. I have the name and birthdate in my pocket. Father Phil wrote it down for me. I don't want to give the constable my only copy. I dodge with, "I will get it right now. Can we meet tomorrow, perhaps when you are off duty? It has to be during the day because I have to be in the hostel by 6:00 or I lose my spot here."

The constable replies, "I am off tomorrow. I will meet you in the downtown park, Victoria Park, at 10:00."

I dash down the hall and photocopy my piece of precious paper. Returning I give it to Constable Jim Kane and agree, "Tomorrow at 10:00, Victoria Park."

After a sleepless night, excited, I am in the park, early. Constable Jim is prompt, right on time, 10:00. He looks quite different in his regular clothes, out of uniform. Unshaven, in a T-shirt and jeans, he is a very handsome young man. Carrying a folder he sits beside me on the park bench. It is a quiet area at this time of day. Victoria Park is named after Queen Victoria. The sidewalks and grass make the shape of a Union Jack flag if seen from the air. It is an immaculately kept park with large, mature maple trees, benches surrounding a statue in the centre of the park of a Native leader who first helped build the city in the late 1800s. The park is ringed by beautiful old churches from all denominations, Anglican, Presbyterian, United and Catholic. You can see how the park would have been a central gathering place back in the day when there were few or no cars. When you walk the park at night, as a prostitute, it looks quite different.

Today, Jim Kane and I have gathered to resolve an issue of a family nature. Jim looks worried sitting next to me, now I am worried. I am thinking that he has changed his mind and does not want to give me the information.

In a concerned voice he says, "Margaret, this person you asked me to find, he is not a good person. You may not want to find him, at all. If he is your father, you are probably better off having not known him."

I am silenced. Searching for words I say to Jim, "The search was exact?"

"Yes Margaret, exact, no doubt. The full name and birthdate match exactly. This is your father," he replies.

I am silenced. Jim can see my struggle and he offers, "You don't have to look at this file, Margaret. Just tell me, give me the word and I will take this file and I will shred it. Honestly, if it were me, in your position, that is what I would want. Shred it and forget it."

I am silenced. I had not anticipated this dynamic in all my musings, never had I thought of this possibility. I say to Jim, "I have to know. Even if I don't act on the information, even if I don't search or find him, I have to know. I have to know to close this chapter of my life."

Jim is struggling. His tight grip on the file tells me that he is thinking about holding the information back as a way to protect me. This only further peaks my interest. I suggest, "Jim, you are so sweet to have helped me. I know this went against your better judgement to do this. I also know that you took a risk to get this information for me. I am hoping one of two things happens here. One, you put that file down and walk away. I will never tell on you. Two, if this is as bad as you say it is, come with me, to find him."

Now Jim is silenced. He responds, "OK, shredding the file and forgetting the whole thing was not on your list of options. Margaret, I have to tell you, I wanted to help you for a reason. My father left my mother when I was like three years old. I never saw him again. I know that feeling, that feeling of abandonment. It is not pleasant. I will go with you, on the condition that you do none of the searching on your own. You only do it with me."

The sexual agenda of our little relationship is gone. This is not flirting. Jim is really afraid, afraid for me. Whatever is in that file has taken the sexual energy out of Jim's sails. Jim continues, "I found my father. The moment I became a cop, I searched. You could almost say that I became a cop, to find my dad. It was a huge disappointment. He was a huge disappointment. I should have figured that out, without the searching. What kind of man leaves a young mother with a child and never pays child support, never visits, never sends birthday cards, Christmas cards, never comes to a hockey game, a graduation, the first prom? I will tell you who, a loser, that's who. Once a loser, always a loser and that is what I found, a loser. But you are right, I had to search. I had to find. I had to find out for myself. I get it."

Seeing Jim's upset I question, "So where do we begin?"

Jim says, "I suggest we go to my apartment and you can read the file, from cover to cover. You should digest this material before we hit the streets to find this guy. You need to know what you are dealing with." Seeing my hesitation he adds, "No funny business Margaret, I promise."

"Jim, thank-you Jim, but I have another confession to make. I can't read the file. I am illiterate. Can you read the file to me?" I confess.

Jim replies, "Yes, of course I can Margaret."

Chapter Twenty-three

Connect the Dots

Moving towards him I show an equally good recall with, "Constable Kane."

He engages me with, "Hey, sorry about the thing at the shelter. I didn't mean to accuse you of helping that crazy husband get in the shelter. That investigation has been closed. He blew himself up and almost everyone else, with the truck bomb. It is still a funny story. Apparently he shopped for a week to find the right dress. It of course had nothing to do with you. I am glad you are OK."

It doesn't take a woman long to figure out when a man's interest has an overly intense sexual component. The excessively erect posture; chest out; the fixed eyes on the breasts; the swelling lips; the deeper voice; are all clear signals that we are not just passing time. I conclude that young Constable Kane has a less than professional interest in me. I know that he has read my file, my record, from our last encounter. It is not a stretch to think that he knows my history includes prostitution. Men, sexually suppressed, inexperienced men are fascinated with prostitution. They watch pornography and think that it is real sex. Their wild imaginations and a bar of soap are enough to send them into a sexual frenzy as they fantasize about what a professional sex partner would do to them. Constable Kane is in a lather.

As I approach the good constable I put this together with my need to find a certain Jacob William Hammel, my father and I see a possible solution. My own efforts are at a standstill, after Google, I got nothing.

Leaving the park my curiosity is running wild. What could be in that file that would scare this big, strong policeman with a gun? It would have to be pretty bad after all the constables, the young officers, see the worst of the worst on the front line of policing. What could scare such a man?

Jim's apartment is just off the downtown core in a renovated warehouse. It is a loft with beautiful large studio windows, brick walls, and wood floors, perfectly sanded with a shiny urethane covering, cathedral ceilings with large exposed beams. He has some modern art on the walls, collections of framed hockey cards, pictures of what appear to be family and friends in exotic places. The open concept space allows one to see from the living room through a dining area to the kitchen. It is a large space, well furnished with couches, chairs, tables and a big screen television There is an elliptic exercise machine that sits in the corner. And then I see it, mounted on the largest brick wall, a surfboard, a surfboard with my art on it. I wonder if he knows to whom that artwork belongs. He sees me staring at the board and asks, "Do you surf?"

Without removing my glance from the surfboard I say, confidently, "Yes, I do."

I continue, "Do you know what you have there on your wall Jim?"

He replies, "No, not really, I don't surf. I found that at a flea market in Toronto and thought it was cool so I bought it and hung it up there."

I can't resist and say, "Do you have a permanent marker?"

He responds, "I think so, why?"

Impishly, I offer, "I am going to increase the value of your surfboard, considerably."

Curiously he asks, "How Margaret?"

I say, "Come here Jim, it's true confession time. Do you see that symbol there, beside the artwork, the letters MAS. That is me, Margaret Anne Sellars. This is my artwork on that surfboard and when I put my full name on this board, it will be worth $10,000 minimum, to the right collector."

Shocked Jim replies, "Get the fuck out of here, seriously?"

"Yep, seriously, that's me. There is, or was, a world where I was famous, a gifted artist on a little cult-like planet, known as the surfing world. This is so amazing to see my work hung on your wall. Let me sign this and you can impress your friends with having met Margaret Anne Sellars or if you need the cash, sell the board," I reply.

"Seriously, you were, famous? Why are you not living in a mansion, on the beach somewhere?" Jim wants to know.

"That is a long, long story Jim. You will have to read the book some day," I suggest. Signing the board I say, "I will personalize a note to you to further increase the value of the board, but don't take anything less than $10,000."

"That is so cool Margaret, thank-you. I can't believe it, you are famous? That art, that piece is so impressive," Jim offers.

"Today Jim, I am little more than a homeless person, a bag lady, living in a hostel. There is no mansion, or Swiss bank account, just me, trying to sort shit out, trying to find my father to see if that fills in any blanks. But yes there was a time that I was famous. Do you like that art? That art, on that board, lives inside me. At any time, at any moment I can create, that level of art," I clarify.

"Well," Jim offers, "I am no art collector but I saw that board and it struck me as cool. It was pleasing to look at. I bought it as a sort of conversation piece, but the conversation just got way better, thanks. Let's get to it."

Jim opens the file and begins, "Jacob William Hammel. Well first let's deal with the arrest record, charges. This is quite the rap sheet. There are charges of; theft, B&E, vagrancy, petty bullshit when he was a juvenile. But then we have some serious shit here; manslaughter, weapons possession, trafficking narcotics, living off the avails of prostitution, having control of a prostitute and murder. He has done time, lots of time in jail and the penitentiary."

"OK Margaret, brace yourself, here is the double barrel, kick in the guts piece. Are you ready?" Jim offers distressed.

"Wait, wait, no I'm not ready. What's going on here Jim?" I ask.

Jim responds, "Margaret, this is a very bad dude. He was under surveillance by police for a long time, on audio tape wire taps, video tape, even direct undercover surveillance for a time. Remember Margret, he was involved in many, many illegal ventures: prostitution; gambling; trafficking narcotics and he was a hired gun, a killer. There is a lot of paper on this guy and boxes of tapes, surveillance tapes, in evidence. Margaret, are you sure you want the whole truth, the whole story?" Jim asks again.

"Yes Jim, tell me."

"He killed your mother."

There is a long pause and Jim continues, "And he just got out of jail. There is no doubt. He was charged and convicted of killing your mother. Your mother is Doris Sellars right? Well, I can't tell if that was clear at the trial, that he killed your mother, but from the arrest record, the evidence and trial material, Jake Hammel killed Doris Sellars as a hit, over gambling debts."

I interject, "Wait, Jake, you called him Jake, his name was Jake? Is there a picture? I have to see a picture."

Jim offers, "Sure, right here, have a look." He hands me the picture, the mug shot, front and side view and there is no doubt.

Staring at the face, fixed on it I fall to the floor. It's him, Jake, my Jake, my pimp, Jake. I fall to the floor, hyperventilating. I vomit on that beautiful shiny floor, wrenching with disgust.

Next I hear Jim's voice. He is saying, "Margaret, wake up, breath, deep breaths, breathe. It's OK, you are here with me, Jim, what just happened? Who is this guy to you?" Jim is trying to support me.

"Jim, I am sorry. You were right. This is a mess," I offer in a distressed voice. "Jacob, Jake, was my pimp. He recruited me out of a group home when I was just a kid. He took me in. He groomed me, taught me the sex trade and then put me out on the street. Oh my god, I had sex with him, my father, my own father, my own father sold me out for sex with other men. Then, then, he tried to sell me into child pornography, the prick, the son of a bitch almost got me killed by some crazy freak Chinaman."

Jim, trying to be the voice of reason says, "That is awful Margaret. I don't want to disrespect your story or diminish it in any way, but, do you think he knew you were his kid? These guys live disgusting lifestyles. He may have known your mother for all of twenty minutes and never knew that you even existed. This could all be a horrible, horrible coincidence."

"Or not," I suggest. "I have to know. Will you help me find him? I think he knew. I think he knew I was his child. There were some things that always bothered me, for years I obsessed over them. I played and replayed certain events over and over in my head. I left Jake, ran away, to go with my mom. I see it like a full flashback, right now. I can see us all together on the street. Jake and I were out and we ran into my mom. Maybe that was no accident? Maybe my mom knew where I was and wanted to get me away from Jake? We were all in the same place, at the same time, once. There were some odd glances there, between my mom and Jake, pauses. Then Jake sold me to the Chinaman, who tried to kill me. I ran away, to my mother's. Then Jake never came to look for me. Jake beat me over wanting to go with my mom but he never tried to get me back from my mother after I ran away. Why? Jake owned me. I was his property. He could have easily found me and dragged me out of my mother's house. He didn't. I wondered about that, for years. Why didn't Jake come and drag me out of my mother's home? He could have easily found me after I didn't come back from the Chinaman. Jake had a lot invested in me. He would not have just let me go. I have to know."

Jim says, "Maybe Jake thought the Chinaman did kill you or maybe Jake went to jail and couldn't get to you. There may be a lot of reasons. He will be easy to find if he just got paroled from the pen. He has to have an accurate address of record."

I am falling off the edge, there in Jim's lovely apartment, "Oh my God, Jim! What kind of man recruits, sexually assaults, grooms then turns their own daughter out for prostitution? Who sells their own child into prostitution? I am going to be sick again. Where is your bathroom?"

Jim points and I run to vacate myself of this horrible possibility. I heave, repeatedly. Jim comes to give me a towel and comfort me. He says that I don't have to go back to the shelter if I don't want to be alone. I sleep on his couch with night terrors about Jake. Skully is there, taunting me, calling me a cry baby, a sissy, a pussy. She has a plan. She is not afraid. She is up for a challenge. I am not.

Awake in the night I am staring at the large beam above my head. I am imagining throwing a rope over the beam and hanging myself there in Jim's beautiful apartment, but I can't. I can't kill myself in a room where my art work is hung like a masterpiece. I stare at the surfboard and wonder how it all went so badly. How did it all come off the rails? Where did I go wrong? Then I remember, the lawyer, the trust account, the hospitalization. I was never the same after that. Mitch, Rider and Gus built the new Tattoo You. It was beautiful but I was non-functional, my brain fried from Electro Convulsive Therapy and overdosed medications. I was fucked. One day, we were in New York City and I just wandered off. I became that homeless, psychotic person that people step over in the bus station. We were in New York to show my art, at an exhibition and there was a fire. I lost all my art. I am mumbling incoherently to myself. I found heroin and like Picasso drew little pictures for loose change, to get enough money to shoot up. I was an addict, putting any and all substances in my body to destroy my consciousness, alter my cognition, escape from reality. I even managed to kill Skully, or rather, put her in a coma. I stopped listening to my warrior. I shut her up. Instead of chasing the perfect wave I was chasing that ultimate high. I lost some twenty years, high, addicted, jail, treatment centres, only to return to the streets, the crack houses, the parks, the alleyways. I want to get myself together and go back to Mitch, Rider and Gus, but somehow I can't. I have the best of intentions, but I just can't. It's too hard, too complicated, too overwhelming. I try, but, I fail. This is a prime example, my current situation. I go to the women's shelter to clean up and what happens, all hell breaks loose. It is not meant to be, every time I move forward, even a little bit, the world kicks the shit out of me. I am a loser and I deserve to die, but first, I am going to find and kill Jake.

Chapter Twenty-four

Revenge

Revenge is a dish best served cold.
– Marie Joseph Eugène Sue

I awaken to breakfast in bed, or couch in this instance. Jim has made me scrambled eggs, bacon, toast and poured me orange juice. He is so sweet. Seeing that big hulk of a man carrying a tray of food in his bunny slippers touched me, emotionally. I see the essence of my struggle. It is as Bert Grimm described, "Who am I and who am I not?" I could see that Jim was secure in his own skin, confident, clear, honest, grounded, a pure soul. I, on the other hand am confused, guessing, second guessing, lying, lost.

"Margaret, I am so sorry. I could barely sleep thinking about how horrible you must feel. There really aren't words to describe how you must feel. You don't have to do this you know. You can walk away. You have the truth. You have your answer, your story is complete, just walk away, now. There is nothing to be gained by finding your father, by finding Jake. You know who he is. He is an asshole. This is not going to be a glorious reunion of two long lost family members. He is a complete dick and he will only hurt you, again," Jim offers.

Grinning, I say, "You sound like my psychiatrist, Dr. Colby. He would not have used the profanity of course. That would be his advice too, I know it and it is good advice, but, Jim, isn't this like, 'Take my advice, I'm not using it.' If this were your father, would you not close the deal and find him, confront him? I have to close this circle, Jim. I believe, and it may be completely faulty thinking that if I find him and I get my answers I will finally be free." I pause to eat some eggs. Staring at Jim I can see that he is getting some vicarious satisfaction out of this. He knows. He understands. I continue with my explanation. "My grandfather use to say that I was a waste of perfectly good sperm. Well Jake donated that sperm. I have questions and he has answers. I need to know how deep this rabbit hole goes."

Jim offers, "I thought you might say that so I called the police station and got the current address for one Jacob William Hammel. Take your time Margaret, have a shower, I can go and wash your clothes if you like. Then, when you are ready, we can drive over there in my car. He is in Boomtown, in Ivan."

"Boomtown? Seriously, Boomtown? That is too rich. I lived in Boomtown, in Ivan, with my grandfather in the trailer park." I have to shake my head to get the irony out from between my ears. I continue with, "The circle is complete, Jim. I am going home, home to the trailer park, Boomtown, Ivan. It's perfect," I explain.

I take a long, hot shower. It is beautiful. Staring at the ceramic tile enclosure in the fog of the hot steamy water I feel like I am showering for the first time. The hot water pours over me as the liquid soap caresses my body. It lasts forever. I feel like I am washing off more than just dirt, soap, shampoo. I feel like I am cleansing my soul. I feel like today will be a changing day for me. Stepping out of the shower and wrapping myself in the warm white towel I see myself in the bathroom mirror. I drop the towel to examine myself fully naked in the foggy mirror. My tattoos are sensational works of art. I hold out my arms and spread my legs to see my cutting scars, my suicide attempts. It has been a long roller coaster ride of a life and I can see the end of the ride in sight. I can see the end of the ride and its name is Jacob William Hammel.

In the bathrobe Jim left me I sit in front of his big screen television and surf through the one hundred and fifty channels of high definition. The fine young man is out doing my laundry. Jim's young life is in great shape. He has a great career, an awesome apartment, friends, and family I conclude. He doesn't need this shit. He doesn't need my shit. I will only contaminate his wonderful life with my toxic waste bullshit of a life.

I run up the stairs to his bedroom area that overlooks the living room. I find and put on a pair of sweats, a T-shirt, socks. Grabbing the file from the coffee table I put on my knife and leave stepping into my shoes at the front door. I have about forty-five dollars in cash. Hailing a cab I give him the piece of paper with the address on it. In a quick twenty minutes I am standing in front of the entrance to Boomtown.

It looks the same. It looks like it did when that little girl stood in this very spot and looked back to see if her grandfather's trailer was on fire. There are about fifty trailers in the park. Each in a decaying state of filth having swallowed poverty, abuse, neglect, addiction, violence, they are the minimum requirement for an address to get welfare. Jake is in trailer number thirty-eight. The roads in the park are dirt, worn from rain. There is no garbage collection in the park. It smells. There is garbage everywhere, dirty laundry hanging off of phone wires, old broken down cars, piles of tires, children's toys and rats scurrying from trailer to trailer. Just as I take my first step into the park I hear a car scream to a stop behind me. Turning around I see that it is Jim. He is pissed jumping out of his car.

"Margaret, you are not doing this alone," Jim shouts.

"No, Jim, you don't have to do this with me. I can do this alone. I want to do it alone." He does not move. We have an awkward pause, a brief Mexican stand-off and I say, "OK, Jim, I tried, but if you insist, let's go." I move to walk into the park.

I was actually happy to see Jim, relieved. He is like the little brother I never had. I thought he might chase after me, or rather I hoped he would chase after me.

"Margaret, you look like a little kid in my sweats and shirt. They are way too big." Jim offers to try and lighten the mood.

"Perfect, Jim, because that was the look I was going for. The last time I was here, I was ten years old, so best I look about the same for my glorious return," I offer, shaking.

Jim sees my anxiety and says, "Let's be cool here Margaret. We are just here for a friendly visit. Nothing stupid is going to happen here. He is on parole. I am a cop. He won't do anything foolish. I will show him my badge and you can get what you need out of him. OK? Are we on the same page? Let's get the answers to your questions and then get the hell out of here," Jim suggests.

Honestly, I had not thought of that approach, that option. I was loaded for bear, ready to slash and burn, with my knife, but Jim's idea is a good one too.

As we walk through the trailer park there is an eerie silence. It's about ten o'clock in the morning. Jim and I are silently glancing around looking at the numbers on the mail boxes or pinned to the aluminum siding on the trailers. We are counting down, 46, 44, 42, 40 and there it is, number 38.

It is an inconsequential little structure like most of the trailers in the park. It is an awful yellow aluminum colour with small sliding silver windows on the sides and both ends. There is a small sidewalk made of slabs of concrete leading up to an aluminum screen door. The trailer is silent, no music, no television playing. Jim steps to the door in a police type defensive posture and looks in the trailer, both directions. Then, he knocks and calls, "Jake, Jake Hammel." There is no response.

Then I see him. He is walking up the road from where we just came, carrying a newspaper. He is in a pair of pyjamas, just the bottoms. He is wearing no shirt or shoes. He is a skinny, bald, gruff looking old man, not the terror I remember. He looks pretty much pathetic. He has his share of prison tattoos, on his arms, hands and chest. It is terrible work, usually done out of boredom to oneself with poor ink and poor tools. His unshaven face has a large scar just below his right eye, but it is, without a doubt, Jake, my pimp, my dad.

Seeing us, standing at his trailer, he calls out in an abrupt belligerent manner, "Who are ya and what do ya want?"

His vision must be poor but once within ten feet I can see it on his face, he knows who I am. Walking past us he mumbles, "Skully, you came home."

Jim, taking control of the situation, showing his badge says, "Jake, may we come in for a chat? I am with the Allentown police."

Jake replies, "Do you think we can't tell a cop when we see one out here in Boomtown? What do you want? I ain't dirty."

Jim offers, "Just a chat Jake."

Jake holds open the door to his trailer and we walk in. It is a filthy pigsty of a mess. We shuffle to a small dining area with a drop-down table and sit.

Jake, sitting across from me says in a raspy voice, "I knew this day would come. I knew you would be here sitting across from me, looking for answers. A man can't live the life that I have and not have a day or two of reckoning. I heard you was dead Skully but obviously I was misinformed."

"Jake, do you know who I am?" I ask.

"If you mean, do I know that you are my kid, yup, I know that. If you are here for back child support I'm all tapped out at the moment," he replies with a mischievous grin.

That was easy considering the weight of the question, a straight up admission.

"Did you know that when Carolyn got me out of the Hippie's Group Home?" I ask.

"Also a yes Skully," he replies. "And before you ask, yes I knew your mother from the time you were conceived to the time I shot that bitch. Listen, I did my time for that. It ain't no secret. The loan shark came to me, paid me five grand, and I killed her, shot her in the face."

"Jake, you had sex with me, you turned me out to the streets, you sold me to other men, for sex," I angrily offer.

"I know that Skully. I am not proud of it, but I did it, knowing you were my kid and all of that. I ain't father of the year. What do I know from parenting?" he answers.

"Why? How?" I demand.

There is a long pause. Jake is shaking his head, ringing his hands. "Survival Skully, you know it, you've done it, things you ain't proud of, to get by, to eat, to live, to stay alive. You killed the Chinaman, right? To survive, him or you, dog eat dog. Don't deny it Skully, you know why. Don't come here with why. It's pathetic. You knew why before you ever came out here," Jake explains. "You look out for number one! Whatever it takes, the code, the code of the street, DTA, don't trust anyone. You've lived it. I know. I have followed your career. I hear things. Did you kill the lesbian Ellen and the crooked lawyer too? Well done, especially that lawyer. He deserved to die. You ain't above it. We are the same you and me. The apple doesn't fall far from the tree. Did you think you were above it all, better than me? Is that what is bothering you? Is that why you are out here? Is that driving you crazy thinking you are more than this? Do yourself a favour Skully, stop tormenting yourself, this is who you are. You are home, accept it. This is your home, Boomtown. You grew up here with your filthy horny old grandfather, right here in this trailer park. You are home where you belong, Skully."

There is a long pause, my eyes are fixed on Jake. I have no words.

"I can tell by the look in your eyes that you need to kill me too, Skully. I see your rage, your hate, your blame. I can taste it. I have been there and felt that too. I welcome death. Kill me, please and I will thank you. You can do it right now and I won't even put up a fight. We are the same, you and I, suicidal. We don't care life from death. I am just too lazy to do it myself, please do it for me. Take this cop's gun and shoot me in the heart, right now, please. I am tired. I welcome the end. I am a disgusting, putrid excuse for a life, so was your grandfather, so was your mother and so are you. We lie, cheat, betray, fuck one another. We are family. Home is where the hate is! Your grandfather did it, your mother did it, I did it and you have done it. Welcome Home Skully!"

With that Jake starts to laugh. He laughs and laughs, louder and louder. It's a raspy laugh, almost coughing, choking.

Then the laughter is broken with a huge bang! Jake slumps over, dead. Jim has shot Jake dead. The bang is followed by an even louder silence.

Jim and I sit motionless, side by side in the trailer, with dead Jake across from us. It is a truly surreal moment. Then Jim curtly says, "That was the biggest load of crap that I have ever heard."

There is another long quiet pause and Jim adds pensively, "You know what I was thinking Margaret, the whole time that lunatic was talking, rambling on and on? I was thinking about your surfboard, your art. Jake never could have done that. You are not the same people, at all. You are not Jake. He wanted you to be him, but you are not. He wanted to drag you down into his cesspool of a life, but that is not who you are. You are an amazing, talented, warrior. He was being disrespectful to you and I just couldn't take it any more. OK you shot the Chinaman and I shot Jake. We are even. We each have something on the other. We are good, right, safe? Now, let's get the fuck out of here."

I can't move. It's like I am frozen there in that filth of a trailer. We are sitting across from the motionless dead body of Jake, my father. I start my reaction with, "What the fuck Jim? What happened to 'Nothing stupid is going to happen here'?"

There is another pause and I continue with, "Jim, you are the third person that I respect to call me a warrior. Two other men, great men said the same thing about me. Bert Grimm, my tattoo mentor and Dr. Colby my therapist both said that I am a warrior. Why can't I see that?" I am crying. "I see failure. I see loser. I see someone with no moral code. I see a freak."

"Margaret, I am not a psychiatrist and I am not a tattoo guru and this may sound trite but, nobody is perfect and I mean that in the most respectful way. We are all struggling. We all have our demons. We have all made our share of mistakes, not used our best judgement."

"I just shot a man, Jacob William Hammel, to put a name to him. He is slumped over right there across from us, bleeding, dead. That was very poor judgement on my part. I could lose everything over that decision, my job, my income, my apartment. This isn't a movie, with dramatic music, cheap one liners and laugh tracks. I am not Clint Eastwood or Dirty Harry. I had no just cause to kill Jake from a moral perspective. He wasn't threatening us. It wasn't self defence. It was murder, plain and simple," Jim explains.

After a pause Jim continues, "All those things you said, about yourself, the loser, freak stuff. That may all be true but there are other parts to who you are that are also true. You are also an artist, a business person, a friend, a warrior. It's not an either or situation. It's both and. It's not that you are either a loser or a winner. You are both. It all exists inside you. It's all real. And here is the really odd part, the part that is hard to accept. It's all a choice. You decide who you are and who you are not. Stop making excuses, just do it, take responsibility, grow up. No one can tell you who you are. It comes from inside, inside you. Stop blaming mommy. Stop blaming daddy. It's time to grow a pair of balls."

With that, I stand up and move towards the door. I am reflecting on what Jim just said. He is a man wise beyond his years. He is what Bert Grimm would have called, 'an old soul', a man that has lived many lives, seen many things and somehow through his genetics brought it all forward with him. A few days ago I barely knew this fine young man. Now, we have shared a murder, a murder and reflections on life. It's the Oprah show with bloodshed. It all seems so random yet so scripted at the same time. Jim may not know how helpful his words have been. Exiting the trailer, walking towards the street, I am not sure what is next. Jim is quietly walking with me. At his car Jim offers, "Why don't you stay with me for a while Margaret? No pressure, no strings, just get out of the hostel. I am actually not there that much. I have a girlfriend and I stay with her a lot at her house. Take your time to make some decisions, decide on your next move. I have the room in that huge place. If you want to pay me in some way, put something else on my wall, your art. I don't need any money."

We are in Jim's car, quiet, driving to his apartment. Jim breaks the silence with, "Margaret, there is one other revelation for today. I have a confession to make. I didn't know when to tell you this, but it was always my intention to tell you the whole truth. I am a little more invested in this whole thing than you know."

I ask, "What do you mean Jim?"

Jim says, "My mother." I can see that he is holding back tears but he continues, "My mother was Carolyn, Carrie."

Shocked I respond, "Carolyn, Carrie, my Carolyn was your mother?"

Jim confirms, "I am afraid so. I have never really met you until recently but I feel like I have known you my whole life. My mom loved you. She spoke affectionately about you, often. Mom had a deep attachment to you. She told me story after story about your courage, your smile, your art. She said that you drew, sketched, all the time."

Surprised, I ask, "You are speaking of your mom in the past tense Jim. Is she alive?"

Jim responds, "No, she died five years ago of cancer. She made me promise her that I would find you. She made me promise that I would look out for you, protect you, help you. I tried, but I couldn't find you, even with the full resources of the police. You really have lived off the grid Margaret. Then, the shelter thing happened, it put us together. I wasn't at the Salvation Army Hostel by accident Margaret. I was there to meet you, to see you. I am sorry that was so awkward. After I bumped into you at the women's shelter I confirmed it was you and I wasn't sure what to do. I thought that I could lose you as quickly as I found you."

"To me, Margaret, you are a legend. Mom had it hard, no one knows that more than you, living with Jake, the streets. You inspired my mom. You inspired everyone that was in that apartment with Jake. You escaped the clutches of Jake. Everyone controlled by Jake saw you as the one, the leader. I didn't know how to treat you. I want to tell you the whole story, back at the apartment, OK?"

"Of course Jim. I would like that," I respond.

The car radio is on, it's Harry Chapin,

'All my life's a circle;
Sunrise and sundown;
Moon rolls thru the nighttime;
Till the daybreak comes around.
All my life's a circle;
But I can't tell you why;
Season's spinning round again;
The years keep rollin' by.

It seems like I've been here before;
I can't remember when;
But I have this funny feeling;
That we'll all be together again.
No straight lines make up my life;
And all my roads have bends;
There's no clear-cut beginnings;
And so far no dead-ends.'

Chapter Twenty-five

The Circle Closes

As we drive away, leaving the trailer park, Boomtown behind us, I feel different. In my head this was going to end as a murder-suicide. I was going to kill Jake and then kill myself. I was resigned to that outcome. It had a certain poetic justice. It seemed like the only possible outcome. Now, however, the suicide clock has been turned back from midnight. I no longer feel that compulsion. Things are adding up to a different total now. I see other possibilities, other options. Jim has made me an interesting offer. I don't see it as permanent but it could be a stepping stone. I have never worked from a foundation before. I have never had a launching pad to take risks from to come back to. Jim is not putting me in a corner, placing expectations on me, getting all up in my face. This has potential. It is resonating quite differently in my head now.

Entering his apartment Jim says, "Let me give you the full tour. This place is massive. I get it pretty cheap because I am like a built-in security service for the larger warehouse building. When people know a cop lives in a building it makes them feel safe and it tends to keep crime away. I have a gun you know. You have seen the main living area but over here, past the bathroom is another large room that we could call your room. Then, back this way, on the other side of the living room is another room. I had the thought initially, that it would be a games room, you know, pool table, jukebox, pinball, but, with this huge studio window, it could as an alternative, be an art studio, your art studio."

"Margaret, I miss my mom, terribly. There isn't a day that goes by when I don't think of her. They are all good thoughts, memories, her laugh, her smile, her hair. I don't want this to get all weird. It's not like I am trying to replace my mom or anything, but I feel like I have known you my whole life. It would be great if you were part of it, no pressure. You can walk away if you like, but it's important to me that you know, you have this, this option, if you want it," Jim explains and continues, "We have had a busy day. We had breakfast, killed a guy and I don't know about you but I am starving."

I ask, "Jim, I am feeling a little overwhelmed just now. You are amazing. I would like to stay here with you. But first, I have some emotional bills to pay. Can I use your phone? And yes they are long distance calls. I need to call Mitch, Rider and Gus at the tattoo parlour. I left them high and dry. Many years ago I abandoned them, I abandoned myself. I got scared and had a flight response and walked away."

"Of course Margaret, use the phone, use the bathroom, use the television, the sink, the stove, everything, anything. You have no idea how happy you have made me. I am going to go out to get a bite to eat, check in with the girlfriend and I will see you later. You have to meet Meagan, the girlfriend, soon, she is great," Jim says as he rushes out.

With Jim gone, alone, I walk around the apartment. In the studio I am standing in the sunlight. I can see myself working in here, tattooing, designing, drawing, even teaching. As I fantasize about the room I think I should go see Dr. Colby too. He deserves some closure to my story as well. Walking to my room, my bedroom, I feel something I have rarely experienced in my life, safety. I feel safe. There are no alarm bells going off, no red flags waving. I have searched all my sensors, checked all the highly sensitive radar and this feels right. I am finally safe.

I know the Tattoo You phone number by heart. I immediately recognize Rider's voice. He was always the receptionist. I have to play with him, so I disguise my voice, I say, "Hey, I was wondering, I wanted to get a tattoo of Elvis across my whole ass, so my butt crack is his mouth, can you do that and how much will it cost?"

There is a silence and Rider says, "Well, I really can't quote that over the phone. It depends on how big your ass is really … Maggie? Is that you? It has to be you, no one else makes a joke like that. Guys! It's Margaret!"

I am weeping. I can't speak. I hear hoots and howls. Thank God some things never change. Perhaps there has been more stability to life than I was prepared to recognize.

Mitch takes the phone and says, "Maggie, is that you?"

I respond, "Yes, it's me Mitch. I am coming to see you guys. I am better. I am really good. I will be there in a few days and Mitch, I am sorry…"

Mitch says, "It will be great to see you, Maggie."

My next call is to Dr. Colby's office. The receptionist offers me an appointment for 4:00, there has been a cancellation. Back in that familiar waiting room at Dr. Colby's office I feel great. As I walk into his office he has the brightest smile for me. He says, "Screw the protocol, give me a hug." We embrace. It is a solid but professional hug. He adds, "Sit Margaret, tell me, what's been going on. Where have you been?"

I begin, "Too much has gone on to really tell, Dr. Colby, but the outcome is wonderful. I just wanted to come by and thank you. I wanted to thank you and tell you that you made a crazy person well. I am doing really well. I am going to stay here in Allentown for a while. I have a real address, no shelters, no hostels, no dumpsters."

"You offered me respect when I had not earned it, when I didn't deserve it. I was quite disrespectful to you in the beginning and I apologize. You honoured my story and showed me compassion. I am ready for the real world now. I no longer have to hide in shelters, alleyways, dumpsters or crack houses. I know who I am and I am proud of who I am. I no longer need to live a life of shame."

The doctor offers, "Margaret, you did all that, you. I helped, but you did the work. I am proud of you. Live long and prosper, my friend."

And with that I left Dr. Colby's office. He too was one of those rocks, one of those foundation pieces that I didn't see even when I was standing on it.

Back at the apartment Jim is there with Meagan. She is beautiful, Carolyn would have approved. I approve. We eat some Chinese take out, watch some television and laugh. I try the elliptic machine. Clearly there remains part of me that is an athlete. I miss my good friend Gus and our body building sessions. Meagan asks to see my tattoos and plans her own design. I ask Jim for more favours. He is so gracious. Jim knows the system and can get me a birth certificate, a social insurance number and driver's education. He agrees to drive me to Toronto to see the lads at the tattoo parlour and Meagan wants to come too. The drive to Toronto has that feeling of adventure combined with a sense of closure.

It is a glorious reunion, my adopted family. Mitch, Rider and Gus forgive me immediately for disappearing. I walked away from Mitch in New York City, leaving him to clean up a huge mess that

I could not cope with.

As we settle into a conversation Mitch says, "Margaret, you are a rich woman. All your business ideas, your art and ventures have been golden. We have a Web site, we are global, selling designs and your art to shops all over the world. This shop is busy to overflow, the California connection is out of control. We have added skateboards to the surfboard market. Then we have boogie boards, knee boards, trick water skis, it has exploded. You are a legend. You know how art goes up in value when you die, well when you vanished, boom! We are completely legit, with lawyers, accountants, everything above board. And you my dear Maggie, have well over one million dollars in the bank and another million in physical assets as well as income of over $200,000 annually. The building you are in, you own, well we own and you have a twin tattoo shop/home, that you own, in California and a surf shop/home in Hawaii. So now when you want to surf, it's all a business expense, tax deductible. Your art continues to show in galleries and reprints are being sold. The New York thing was pretty easy to clean up. As it turns out we did have insurance because we rented the truck. I had photographed all the work and the insurance company settled our claim."

I am speechless. I had not expected this. I assumed the money had been pissed away, lost or stolen. I have gone from being a homeless person with no fixed address to having four homes, between Allentown, Toronto, California and Hawaii. It is all so overwhelming. Rider breaks the silence with, "Do you want to do a tat?"

Meagan steps up with, "Do me, please? I want that Spartan warrior on my calf."

My booth, my work area, built for me but never really used, sits like a shrine adorned with my art. I sit in my chair for what feels like the first time and get Meagan to lie down on my table. It's like I was never gone, never missed a beat. As I work, Mitch says, "I don't know if you noticed but this building, that you own, that holds our shop, also contains your old apartment. We spruced it up a bit. It was our way of keeping you alive, of believing in you, that you would come back. So now you have a huge, serious, flat panel, plasma screen television with a satellite on the roof, leather couches, oak furniture, a new bed and actual appliances. It's all pretty cool. We don't know what your plans are but, you have a place to live here too."

I am lost in my art working on the Spartan tattoo for Meagan. Other customers are in the shop. It is clearly a thriving business. Tattoos have gone legit, mainstream. It is no longer an underground cult thing. As I finish up with Meagan I say to Jim, "Do you have any holidays you can take?"

Jim answers, "Sure, always."

I add, "What about you Meagan? Can you get off work for a week?"

She says, "Sure, why?"

With my biggest smile I say, "Let's go surfing, the trip is on me."

Landing in Hawaii we are greeted like rock stars by people we don't even know. They are running the surf shop for me, my staff. As we pull up to the shop I see the huge neon sign over the door, 'Maggies Surf Shop'. I have gone from Boomtown, the trailer park, to the beach in Hawaii in less than a week. Life is good. I know who I am and if I forget I can step outside and check the sign above the door. I am Margaret, artist, friend, adopted mother, business owner.

THE END